Half-Bads in White Regalia

Half-Bads in White Regalia

Cody Caetano

&

SHEFFIELD – LONDON – NEW YORK

First published in the UK in 2026 by And Other Stories
Sheffield – London – New York
www.andotherstories.org

1 3 5 7 9 8 6 4 2

ISBN: 9781916751439
eBook ISBN: 9781916751446

Offset by Tetragon, London; Cover Design: Elisa von Randow, Alles Blau Studio, Brazil, after a concept by And Other Stories; Author Photo: © Alex Jacobs-Blum.

And Other Stories books are printed and bound in the UK on FSC-certified paper by the CPI Group (UK) Ltd, Croydon.

A catalogue record for this book is available from the British Library.

And Other Stories' Authorized Representative within the EU GPSR legal framework is: Logos Europe, 9 rue Nicolas Poussin, 17000 La Rochelle, France. (Logos Europe do not represent to publishers the rights to this title.) E-mail: Contact@logoseurope.eu

And Other Stories gratefully acknowledge that our work is supported using public funding by Arts Council.

Supported using public funding by
ARTS COUNCIL ENGLAND

MIX
Paper | Supporting responsible forestry
FSC® C013604

For Zion, Milo, Eli, and Osias

Prologue

THE BUCKLE

Ask any half-bad to tell you the story about how their bad half came to be and they'll probably begin with the buckle.

The buckle is a rumble that hijacks the interior faculties to make one think and act without compunction. The buckle attacks the locus of focus and apes the half-bad's best intentions, only to play them like a chump chimp. And if left unchecked, the buckle will keep going until the frequencies connecting them to community fizzle out into the ether of rumour and myth.

The buckle's kink is myopic stimulus, pitching id toward what one elder warned me against: that "big do, little think" business. And what little I've learned in my meagre years of living is that a half-bad story is always concerned with a big do and the amount of blue the half-bad feels for doing it.

Baddies are different: infamous pros who go the distance. Baddies work in tandem with the buckle, will just mutter fuck it to themselves real quick and not lose any hair over it.

Baddies relish in the wanton swelling of the genitals, nervous systems, fists, and lips, no matter if it costs them a best friend or credit score, or if it breaches what sleeps between armpit and sternum. In the stories baddies tell, the buckle is instinct, and they can't help it. It's the buckle and that was yesterday. Just get over it already.

There are many stories about the buckle royally messing something up, a good chunk of which are so gnarly that most people just send the baddie on their way. Toss the bastards on baddie island. Free ticket on the one-way. As they should. Cuz those stories leave many feeling as though there's no way but the one-way, no getting over it, and we come to them hoping they'll teach us the differences between baddies and the rest of us.

But they also leave some half-bads curious and terrified about the rapid onset of their own buckling, wondering if there's something to be done before the big do comes to usher them from half-bad to baddie. Or maybe it's better to just think of the buckle as a warning attached to every half-bad story, even if the half-bad never warns as such.

PART I

HAPPYLAND

The Eastside of Happyland

Nobody called it Happyland back then. We didn't know Happyland was a thing. But that two-street highway community of ours is most certainly there if you zoom in far enough in Google Maps.

People just called it the house, or Eastside Drive, or Severn (which swallows every highway community within a few kilometres or so). But the internet tells me we lived on the Eastside of Happyland, just across the freeway. And there must be something there if the internet tells you so.

The Eastside of Happyland fits nicely into the plot of Severn, which names a dozen patches of human activity scattered along Highway 11. Not the Queen's favourite land, either: mostly feet-burning, unforgiving turf. Summer so humid it hurts. Burger joint, bathroom break, and pit stop just up the road.

Way before it was called Happyland, a few neechies came to this place and named it Gissinausebing, which the township's website translates as "cold water," back when the nibi was only clean and cool and life-giving and pristine. It's easy to imagine the nigigwag roaming and the neechies loving it there unconditionally for a long time. It's also easy to imagine butterfly towns popping up like chicken pox across Little Miss Dominion, in clusters gathering along the lake, with baddie thoughts of burger stops and disposition inbound. Cuz both things happened. But so did our time living on the Eastside of Happyland.

Before any patches, pox, or burger stops, and even before those neechies took back their grist mill or set those fishing weirs up, the oldest ones on this island, the nibi here went untouched for hundreds of millions of years: pooling into lakes and lolling in lazy rivers that snaked and warmed and expanded and rose with the heat coming from the heartbeat up in the sky.

The Bull and the Old Woman

Before I was born, and before we moved to Happyland, two half-bads named Mindimooye and O Touro rented a three-bedroom townhouse in Toronto's Downsview neighbourhood. And while I have about zero memories of them ever getting intimate, mind a brief kiss during *Fear Factor* or a good-job-baby embrace after watching me beat the opening boss on *Star Fox 64*, they most certainly did a big do one awfully hot and soggy mid-August day in 1994. Cuz nine months later Mindimooye rushed her butt over to Women's College Hospital when she broke water. Said I came out in no time flat and with an obstructed intestinal tract that made me gassy and colicky. She named me after Mel Gibson's kid in *Tequila Sunrise*, which I've never watched and don't plan on watching anytime soon, thank you very much. But just picture colicky me and Mindimooye getting plenty sick back then. Ziplocked ice cubes melting in pellets down her crown and the constant rhythm of pinching and twisting the lids off medicine bottles. Got this sick with my big brother, Julian, too. Rightfully blames the cartons of cigs and cough antibiotics, even remembers calling poison control one time. Anything to kick those vise-grip headaches and fevers that wouldn't quit. Sometime around then I got dropped on the head, which explains a bit.

Like plenty, O Touro and Mindimooye got sick of living in the city. Cuz cities make people sick sometimes. Besides, O Touro had always wanted to leave and try raising his family on a river. Something to offer me and Julian and our big sister, Kristine. Cuz O Touro would swim as a fish if he could.

When Mindimooye got a job as a server at Casino Rama, making seven dollars an hour plus infinite tippage, she and O Touro went looking for a house around there. They wanted the bush but settled for half-bush. (If you can still hear the highway, you're not in the bush.)

One of the casino bartenders who sometimes flirted with O Touro told them about this four-bedroom, two-floor house at the maw of a marshy forest that faded into leafy darkness. Granny suite on the bottom floor. Just a fifteen-minute drive from Sunshine City and Casino Rama, too. Rural route number three.

Neither of them minded the house's occasional history of family-breaking. But their real estate agent did mention the previous owners when asked, including one claptrap couple who went through the nastiest and noisiest divorce in the county shortly after moving in. Never mind the families before them, too. I've always wondered if it was the house that broke the family or the family that broke the house. Maybe that's why they got it so cheap.

Nobody knew about the swamp until long after we moved in. Sure, the previous owners had already solved a few of the plumbing problems by adding filtration systems and installing a reverse osmosis system under the kitchen sink so whoever lived there had a drinking source. Yes, the current divorcing owners' cats left a batch of fleas as a housewarming gift, but the new ones wanted the house too much to give a crap. O Touro wanted the pool table, the lawnmower, the blinds, all of it.

So in 1997, the five of us moved into Happyland with help from some aunties and uncles. And it wasn't too long before O Touro began building a debarked cedar fence around the perimeter, right before the front and backyards dipped into a channel moat that would fill with slush during the many stormy days and nights to come.

Saudade

It didn't take long for the house in Happyland to become a place for tented backyard gatherings and celebrations, for dozens of family friends, cousins, aunties, and uncles to stay over and take needed weekend breaks and staycations. I grew up thinking a home is the noise a house can't make.

I'd wake up early and find bodies on couches, mind an adult or two chatting in the kitchen or the dining room or smoking out front on the scorching porch steps. There was plenty of hollering and busting through a few too many two-fours of Bud or Canadian, shooting pool under bulb and moonlight, cig smoke oozing from the back porch until the heartbeat broke over the trees and the faint hum of the radio greeted the morning dew. There were casino parties and birthday parties and anniversary parties and wedding parties and Halloween parties and Christmas parties and Canada Day parties and reunion parties and there was always a reason to have people over. These were the first times I ate pizza or got to stay up late chasing cousins through the legs of the adults.

Even as a sick newborn who Mindimooye came to adore as "Boo Bear," my brother quickly developed into a skinny yet active mama's boy who carried handfuls of swirling energy every day, so much so that O Touro and Mindimooye watched VHS tapes about attention deficit disorder and brought him to the doctor for an assessment. He never did get that diagnosis, though. And over time, that raw energy slowed into a deliberate and sensitive calmness. I once heard someone call him "the turtle of turtles." But back in Happyland, Julian had no shell, and I understood him as a loyal, no-bullshit tour guide for the many realms and worlds of our youth that came to us in plastic compact discs and over the satellite dish. Having someone so finely attuned to a rotation of fantasies made them even more believable to me.

In home videos, Mindimooye is always pushing Kristine on a city park swing or filming her running along a sidewalk or beach, and in those videos Kristine is just a little sweetie with two honeypot eyes, a baby so cute that Mindimooye put her in contests and pageants. Put her in swimming lessons, too, cuz Mindimooye almost drowned as a little girl. Kristine knew how to dive in if we fell overboard.

As the oldest, my sister developed her brother-sitting chops early. By age ten, Kristine was making five bucks to watch me and Julian, changing two-year-old me's diapers and making us food before Mindimooye woke up at noon. Before she became the family thunderbird, swooping in to protect us from the buckle, she was a blur out the door to classmates' birthday parties at Cinema Four or to hang out at the food court at Sunshine City Square Mall, going to YMCA dances and trying to set her friends up with the boys at Notre Dame Catholic, hitting her crushes with a "GTG" on MSN Messenger whenever someone shouted at her to set the table for dinner. But when Mindimooye and O Touro went out for the day, Kristine often snuck into Mindimooye's closet to stare at a much-cherished film camera, fingers gliding over the switches and cranking the lens and bringing the viewfinder to her eye to find a new perspective on things.

As for me? I was the baby of the family, always overflowing bowls of Cheerios and Lucky Charms onto the vinyl tablecloth and the floor cuz I poured the milk in first. Mindimooye always cut up my hot dogs and never let me near scissors or knives. Not to mention I had a tendency to take off, by tricycle or by foot, across the backyard and the adjacent cul-de-sac, a dirt circle that sometimes doubled as a small parking lot for visitors if too many cars sardined in our driveway. This tendency was exploited one day when the boy across the street pulled up on his bike while I was playing with Bear, the family golden retriever. His parents and their kids looked like *Caillou* cartoons, so I'll call him Caillou.

"Why don't you go in and hide?" he said, pointing to the forest. "I'll count to sixty and then come find you."

Caillou was a few years older than me, so I naturally did what he asked. Together we walked right up to the maw of the forest and stood there waiting for Donkey Kong or a throng of raptors to come barrelling toward us, but nothing came. So I waved him off on his bike and ventured into the unknown with Bear, who carried whatever hunk of rock he got that day with him in his mouth.

Bear and I started strong. I'll give us that. I kept to what little of the trail I knew until I couldn't see the maw anymore, losing all confidence and sense of direction. Then I kept going some more. It wasn't until after an hour or two of walking that I realized I was lost. We circled the woods until Bear's intuition took us back to the maw, right as O Touro came marching from the yard. He pulled my pants down and spanked me two or three times. It was the only time he ever hit me.

Goat Belly

As we often did, the five of us crowded in the family car to visit Uncle Rob and Uncle Bill, who ran a show-dog farm out in the pastures of Elmvale, on the way to Wasaga Beach. They raised German shepherds for buyers and area competitions. Uncle Rob's dogs won championships and first-place ribbons cuz he understood the shepherds enough to be one. The loud ones got names like Thunder and the ones who acted up got names like Asshole and Fuckhead.

We went over a bridge that broke through a thicket of willows and snoring Entings as Mindimooye explained once again from the front seat: "They've got dogs, chickens, goats, couple turkeys, barn cats, lots more. Just beyond the bridge. You'll see, my love."

We drove past cattle-crowded fencelines and fields of dandelions behind them. As we pulled up to the house, I could see a chimney-red brick: the type of farm to get painted and framed above a bed-and-breakfast toilet. Stink of dung billowed into our windows, so we rolled them up and got out to unload the weekend junk from the trunk.

We parked in the front, and just beyond us was glorious scrap metal, unfinished projects, and piles neglected entirely. But also stray cats. And the greenest of grass. Butterflies. It was clear no one was worried about changing things anytime soon. Young and old alike could get lost for hours exploring out there.

Arrhythmic barking came in a vivid sonic wave from skinny kennels jutting out the front of the house. I could see only two or three kennels but heard at least a dozen shepherds thundering at us from around the corner. As the barking got out of hand, a dark, handsome man with an acorn head, cleft chin, and pothead's cough came into view wearing muddy boots and sweatpants, telling them mutts to shut the fuck up. He came over for a magnificent hug, calling me Code Monster, asking Mindimooye where his kiss was at, so good to see you guys, damn mutts don't ever shut up, eh?

Uncle Rob helped us carry bags to the back door. He and Bill didn't want anyone coming through the front and disturbing the sweet little nativity scene of newborn pups that had arrived the previous night. Uncle Bill came out in minty vet slacks, as pale as Uncle Rob was dark, telling Code Monster that no hug means no dinner.

By the time we were unpacked, the adults had bid us kids to go play out back while they made dinner. Julian and Kristine walked me to the edge of the farm and pointed to the distant woods beyond the fence, past the dried grasslands dotted with the odd haystack Uncle Rob and Uncle Bill had tossed after they quit selling cattle, a land where horses once trotted and munched on the bale. They took me to hissing turkeys and koi fish chilling in a rock pond. They took me to play hide-and-seek with the baby billy goats that roamed freely through the half-bush. They brought me ducklings until their mama got pissed and chased us long after we put them back and said sorry. We saw kitties breastfeeding and blind Siamese mew-mews rolling around the straw-packed loft of the barn or in the garage, and my big siblings told me the uncles had an extra kitty for us that we weren't allowed to take home cuz Mindimooye's lungs puffed up around cats, especially Siamese ones.

For dinner, we ate tasty ham or turkey and cobs of corn, mashed potatoes, and steaming broccoli with a sliding hot square of butter on top. I spread the shepherd's pie around in a figure eight, and Uncle Bill licked his plate clean. There was a metal kennel in the corner of the dining room with a shepherd named Kelly in it. Kelly's eyes glowed and shimmered like supple green Jell-O in the light as he watched me eat dinner.

"Uncle Rob? I got a question."

"Yeah?"

"Why d'you keep Kelly caged up like that?"

"Kelly is caged up cuz he's a stud magnet, Code Monster. People pay big bucks to mate their females with that one. But we keep him locked inside at night cuz one day when we were out Kelly smashed through the front windows to get at a female in heat."

"Sounds just like your old man," O Touro said, probably.

After dinner and a few stories, we played Risk and ate brain-freeze bowls of Neapolitan ice cream, our socks in our shoes at the door. Some time passed after O Touro or Julian conquered the world cuz the adults migrated like always to the tempered-glass patio table out back, screen door eerrrrreeerrreerring for the rest of the night, a case of Bud crinkling, Rock 95 I-Love-Rock-n-Roll-ing, and a mosquito coil ember they gathered around.

At midnight, we watched pay-per-view *Alien* on the lower level of the house and snacked on tins of butter cookies. I remember crawling through Uncle Rob's mini-forest of houseplants and finding some unlucky mouse in a trap. Beetles trotted along the plush off-white broadloom. Pretty soon, we fell asleep and occasionally woke to the snap of the screen door, followed by one of our farmer uncles screaming you mutts better shut the FUCK up real soon cuz some of us need to get up at the cockle doodle doo.

The next morning, I woke on a waterbed upstairs. All the bedrooms were empty, and as I got downstairs I could hear a nearby hacking. I followed the sound out back toward the barn. In the distance, I saw Uncle Rob and O Touro standing underneath a splayed pink mass tied by the hoof to the branch of a tree. The other three hooves hung slunk to the ground, and they went at it laughing, smokes in their mouths, having a blast and taking turns hacking out chunks of the belly with cleavers and gravity. They hacked so loud they didn't hear me coming around the corner. A couple strips had missed the bucket and splattered the grass with the blackest of blood. It was the blood that came from the belly. It was the first time I saw anything's intestines and needed zero permission to be terrified about my own organs and insides.

I stayed looking for a moment too long before turning around and pretending I never saw it. And then the two of them and the belly split off and the brain pic switches to an image of a foregrounded fence, where there are three goats instead of four standing behind it, and I'm grabbing at chunks of my stomach.

Walmart Plaza

The first time I saw Mindimooye cry was shortly after we parked among a herd of trucks, Civics, and soccer vans that had funnelled into Walmart Plaza, a new development at the bottom of the West Ridge burbs in Sunshine City. Mindimooye had already killed the engine, air-con, and Rock 95, but remained buckled up in driver, just staring at the rain dripping down the windshield. She let go of the wheel, released her seat belt, and began shivering like she'd just eaten a Hungry-Man out of the box. Hadn't spoken more than a sentence or two all morning. I wasn't much older than five, maybe six.

We were at Walmart Plaza cuz I missed the bus again. Before the other supervisor on Mindimooye's shift got it out for her, enough to get her canned from Casino Rama, she spent many of her nights supervising the beverage graveyard shift. Sometimes I'd wake up in the middle of the night and find her seated in front of the TV or planted on the basement carpet, glasses on and hair bundled in a scrunchie, pairing socks to *Dances with Wolves*, and we'd share a smile. "Back to bed, babe. What you doing up this late?" She wouldn't move from the spot until I nudged her out of a soft snore the next morning, the special features menu looping infinite on the screen.

That morning I went up to Mindimooye and poked her awake with the keys, rubbed her shoulder best I could, told her I missed the bus. She rolled over and told me to start the car.

Whenever we drove to school late, a sheet as cloudy as tap water flattened the county skyline and set the tone for signing in, coat and sneakers still soaked from the day before. Believing that the weather mocked our frequent lateness didn't change the truth that driving somewhere late with your family, with all its coded anger, swear-at-the-bank-drive-thruing, and omission, was the kind of ride where everybody inside sat clenched for the next yellfight but never got the relief of having one. Or you got something like it but didn't know.

Mindimooye never did much crying back then—least not in front of me—so I began asking her questions like, "What you doing?" and "Mom?" but she was heaving too hard to say anything back, and could muster up nothing more than "Your dad is a bad man."

Flopping Around in My Head

Mindimooye and O Touro got married in 1985, while they were living on the top floor of a semi-detached house in Toronto.

"I'm at home and breastfeeding your sister," Mindimooye tells me the other day. "I finally had enough money to rent a car. He stumbled back in after going missing for a few days and said, 'I'm here to play Dad.' 'Okay,' I said, 'let's try this again.' He'd ask me, 'What do you need? Do you need something? Tell me.' That night, he runs to the store to get milk. 'I'll just take the car.' Half-hour goes by. An hour. Two hours. I go and try to find him. One day. Two days. I take your sister down to somewhere on St. Clair West. I track him down. Where was he? Doing crack at some whore's apartment. Fucker thought it was okay to steal my car. He was just gonna get milk, Cody."

A couple years later, when Mindimooye was pregnant with Julian, she was in a low place. Sometimes I think that's why Julian got so sick as a baby. She was a bundle of nerves and didn't know what was wrong with her, and if it wasn't for the Boo Bear growing in her belly, she said she would have taken her life. It wouldn't be until much later that she got angry about everything, when she was done getting smacked around.

One day, O Touro needed to borrow the car again. He kept telling Mindimooye he needed to pick up some things and had to go right away. She told him no, she would drive, cuz that way she'd know exactly where the car was. So she dropped him off wherever he had to go and left the car running. Kristine was just a toddler in the back seat. And then before she knew it, O Touro came running out of the house with two random dudes, all three of them carrying black garbage bags, and they screamed at Mindimooye to get the fuck out of there and drive c'mon go go go.

Before I was born, Mindimooye and O Touro took Kristine and Julian to Disney World for a week. There are photos of O Touro posing with baby Julian on a surfboard, at the rented trailer in Florida, in the bars doing karaoke. O Touro still has his shaggy, filled-out mullet. Mindimooye's hair is massive, and they're both decked out in neon and funky camouflage. Mindimooye's mom, my nana Flo, is like a phantom presence, always in the background of group photos, around tables at bars, never smiling. Maybe cuz the buckle came on the first night of the trip.

"It was easily the scariest thing I've ever seen," Kris says. "Watching him beat the shit out of her, her hiding behind me, begging him to look at me, 'Not in front of her, please,' just trying to make him stop it for my sake. Remember I'm only three, and this guy is just Dad, you know? But he's got her cradled into a ball behind me. Nana's watching with Julian in her arms and we're crying at once, begging for him to stop."

"It's his trademark," Julian says. "He can make the happiest place on earth turn into the most terrifying. And he can do it just like that." He snaps his fingers.

On the second night of the trip, O Touro locked Mindimooye and Kristine in the trailer bedroom. They held their pee for hours. Around dawn, Kristine heard Nana Flo in the main room, screaming "Can't do this shit no more, O Touro. Can't do this shit!"

Kristine peeked through the crack of the bedroom door and saw Nana Flo and O Touro outside. Eventually he passed out and began snoring, and they snuck to the bathroom to pee.

At this point Mindimooye knew that it was her children who were keeping her alive, but she also felt cuz of her own childhood that her kids needed to know their father. She didn't want them to feel alone. She didn't want to do it alone. They moved rapidly to two apartments over the course of two years. At the second, O Touro abstained from using and got in counselling for anger management and substance abuse.

Like plenty, the treatment didn't work for O Touro. Never did back then. All twenty-plus attempts and counting. But when O Touro came back and hit her again, she'd saved up enough paycheques and tips for first and last and bit by bit began to move into another apartment, above a gun shop.

Mindimooye would take Nana Flo's car at night, whenever O Touro was out. She officially left after he disappeared for a couple days. Her friends would always laugh about the irony of Mindimooye sneaking away and relocating on top of a gun store.

When I google the address now there's no gun shop, just an H&R Block next to a Victory Tabernacle of Jesus Christ banner in the window next to a hair salon that hid lollipops under the chair when they cut Julian's ninja-inspo ponytail into a fierce mullet and an official restraining order was registered with the cops.

Mindimooye got a job at a place called Angelo's to support Kristine and Julian. She lied to O Touro and said she worked at the Novotel. He went around, asking mutuals where she was and where she'd moved to. Went to the Novotel. Nobody knew.

Maybe he recognized her car parked outside. Maybe someone, one of my aunties or uncles, told him where she stayed by accident. Mindimooye doesn't know how he got there. But O Touro found their apartment and an alleyway brick, and whipped the latter at the former, right through the living room window.

On another night that year, he stopped by when Mindimooye was on a serving shift at Angelo's. Nana Flo was babysitting like always and had opened the door by accident. And that's when the buckle came for O Touro.

Kristine and Julian share a brain pic of him standing in the dark living room bathed in television blue. Nana Flo kept asking what he was doing there, and O Touro kept screaming at Nana Flo, demanding to know where Mindimooye was. Again and again.

Then he picked up this granite statue—"Aztec Man," Julian calls it—and hurled it at a fish tank Mindimooye saved up a couple paycheques to buy, sent the foot-long suckerfish thrashing into shattered glass, burying itself in the wet carpet.

Julian and Kristine began crying and Nana Flo began screaming, some tiny fish still inside the aquarium choking on the air like reverse *Titanic*, the others bouncing on the carpet.

After the hallway light flipped on, O Touro had to jet before the cops showed up. The cop came in with a flashlight and cast it across the room, and then four of them were cleaning up, putting the family suckerfish and the other ones into cereal bowls, waiting for Mindimooye to finish her shift. Julian says the cop looked like she was used to it.

Still, O Touro didn't learn any lessons from that night. On another he climbed the fire escape as he'd done before. He scaled the roof, peeked inside the windows, and saw Mindimooye in there sleeping with my sister, who was still way too young for what was about to happen. Back then, O Touro was in shape and incredibly flexible.

The sound of the window sliding open woke Kristine up, and she saw him crawl through it and then slither down Mindimooye's bedroom wall. His bodyweight hitting the floor shook Mindimooye awake. Instinctually, Mindimooye and Kristine got up and ran and made it to the bathroom in the hall before he caught up to them. The screaming began and Kristine huddled to the ground and covered her ears. All she saw was flailing legs and struggling and then suddenly her face met Mindimooye's after she dropped to the floor, lifeless. That's the word Kris wants me to use.

O Touro then dragged Mindimooye to the room and locked the door. Kristine banged on it for however many minutes it took for him to odooditinaan. My sister sat there screaming and pounding until she heard the lock unclick.

She barged in, only to find O Touro slithering back up the wall and Mindimooye naked on the bed. She cradled her as the bruises began to bloom.

After that, Kristine began to have recurring nightmares. In one, she's on the sidewalk with Mindimooye and Julian and they're running away from a giant skeleton. But always in the dream she knows it's them two slowing Mindimooye down, cuz she has to run while carrying all their coats and boots. In another, she sees O Touro's shadow by the bottom of the cement staircase at their old apartment, and as he slowly walks up the stairs it grows bigger and bigger, and Mindimooye is knocked out on the futon and wrapped in blankets.

"But maybe that one wasn't a dream," she says. "I was so scared of him. There was an association with violence, and that's why I'd panic every time they kissed. And I'd lose my crap on Mom and she'd go, 'I got back together with him for you guys.' But she didn't, she brought him back for herself."

When they first got back together, my sister woke up to Mindimooye's roaring laughter and then walked down the hall to see the television casting that same blue light over the living room. She was still half-asleep when she saw them on the sofa. Mindimooye was naked and had a thin sheet draped over her. O Touro has hair still in these brain pics, but Kristine didn't know who O Touro was, really.

They tried to shoo her back to bed. But she was upset and didn't want to leave Mindimooye. Kristine was too angry to see him. Every time his fingers touched Mindimooye's body, she thought it gave her a bruise.

"When you're a kid, it's hard to distinguish dreams from reality," Julian says. "At least the little details blur together. I still have that suckerfish flopping around in my head. It left a stain inside my stomach. It feels like a little black hole that I fall into every time I think about it."

O Touro breached his restraining order multiple times, came back from treatment twice, and kept routine checkups at a halfway house, where he chose to go instead of jail. Mindimooye got pregnant with me while living in the apartment above the gun shop. Kristine resented Mindimooye for bringing O Touro back. "I hated him back then for what he did to her," she says. "And then she got pregnant and there was a baby. The baby was you."

O Touro began balding and shaving his head after they moved to the Downsview house. Things seemed to get better. He built a massive garden with an array of brilliant flowers and Mindimooye painted the living room tangerine. It was there that Mindimooye dropped me on my head by accident cuz she was doing too much laundry in one arm with me in the other. She thought she killed me. But here I am.

The Catacombs

In the 1990s, a minister granted domestic adoptees like Mindimooye access to the registry to let them search for their birth parents with the help of a horribly bureaucratic system. At some point, an adoptee goes looking through their family history and charts for possible biological links, cheat codes, the bluest of clues. Some adoptees got lucky after the opening of the catacombs. Other adoptees not so much.

Mindimooye didn't want to look at first, and it took a while for her to even get past the fear of spoiling her father's memory or hurting Nana Flo's feelings. But after the buckle came she said Fuck it, I want to know. She banked on the excuse that she needed to learn her medical history and jumped in.

She wrote her first-ever letter to the Adoption Disclosure Unit in the summer of 1990, shortly after Julian was born. She found the time to write the letter out by hand, with a request both earnest and keen, seeking "any and all" deets Little Miss Dominion had regarding the stork basket. Any details Nana Flo bothered to share got attached to the back of the letter. She manila-enveloped it out.

In October she received a confidential letter that regretted to inform her they had little information to share and that prior to 1979 the collection of social history was not a requirement in private adoption placements. It went on to say that most mothers chose adoption for their baby cuz they "did not have the financial resources or community support needed to give the baby a good start in life." That or they freaked out about the taboo surrounding babies born out of wedlock, so much so that they sometimes neglected to even tell the O Touros, who had no legal rights back then anyways, who sometimes didn't do anything if the mother told them. This did not discourage Mindimooye.

At the start of the following year, an assistant clerk notified her that the request had finally been processed and entered into the ministry's catacombs, which they called "The Register." They told her that no birth parents had registered before then and that they'd only just begun conducting searches for those who registered in 1986. Welcome to a four-year waiting list.

More than two years later, the ministry mailed her an affidavit in support of the application that she had to get notarized with a commissioner's seal, with a fifteen-dollar fee payable to Little Miss Dominion's minister. She could expect to wait four to six weeks upon mailing it out for the letter to process.

By November of 1993, Mindimooye had received a copy of her adoption order.

It took three years for the Adoption Disclosure Unit to tell her that she should check back in eighteen months if she hadn't heard anything.

Even after we'd moved to the house in Happyland, Mindimooye looked with any spare time she had between O Touro, us three kids, and casino shifts. But Little Miss Dominion got snappy.

About a year later, a patronizing letter was sent on behalf of the Register to Mindimooye, who had just completed her Search Information Form. They mentioned it could take nine more months from the receipt of the form, then two to three months after that. They told her to stop calling.

And then sometime between 1998 and 2000, they found her mother's name and birth date, and Mindimooye's new last name. I remember the look on her face when she saw her new name on the computer screen. I remember her saying it out loud. She didn't turn around when I stood in the doorway. She didn't take her eyes off the screen.

Something shifted in Mindimooye after she discovered that new name of hers. Something did. Even though it was her old name. Even though she'd been through a couple name changes already. Even though it was her name all along.

Booster Pack

Little Miss Dominion said All right, sorry about that. Here's your card. It was, of course, the ultimate certificate of residency, that red plastic card to confer membership to a different registry altogether.

Mindimooye completed an Application for Registration of Children Under the NDN Act and faxed it out, applying for me, Julian, and Kristine at once. O Touro signed it too. At the advice of NDN and Northern Affairs, she wrote a letter in Comic Sans to the Revenue Agency, slipping in how happy she was to learn what "the government did not allow to be disclosed back in the 1960s," as a Native baby born in the sixties. Plus after four long years of serving and paying wage taxes at Casino Rama, she had some questions.

The office told her she could collect for as far back as 1985. Knowing Little Miss Dominion, I bet anything more would just be getting greedy. But she doesn't know how resourceful my family is. Mindimooye wanted to know if she would also receive the PST from back when that was still around. PST on goods purchased, on withdrawals of RPPs, on property tax. On tuition. Imagine all the PST you paid over the course of fifteen years coming back at once. Wouldn't suck, would it?

I didn't really understand what had happened. But suddenly, albeit briefly, a fat stack of income tax she got back while living at the house in Happyland came and signalled unprecedented economic stimulus for us all.

It distracted them from an ongoing credit crisis. O Touro, who got canned from his job at the casino and shifted to labour and construction after getting his truck driver's licence, bought a gargantuan plasma-screen TV that we collectively dubbed "The Plasma," a dining room table, a computer, a stereo system, a load of Leon's furniture, and a truck. They started spending like crazy when she got all that money back and bought more than they could afford. Mindimooye bought Julian bunk beds and a PlayStation One Mini with *Gran Turismo 2* and *Spyro 2: Ripto's Rage!* They repainted the rooms of the house. We celebrated some more. But what started out as a brief period of happiness as a collective unit also happened to be the beginning of the end of Happyland.

Is

Mindimooye met Alice on one of her casino shifts in the fall of 2000. Like plenty, Alice came to Casino Rama for the slots. Like plenty, Alice asked Mindimooye what nationality she was.

"I said something like, 'I think today I'll be French.'"

That made Alice laugh. That was how one made money at the casino: chatting with the regulars and getting them to laugh.

Alice later revealed to Mindimooye that she'd started her own private registry out of Barrie for adoptees disappointed by Little Miss Dominion's. She'd given up her own daughter a long time ago. After a few conversations, Alice asked Mindimooye if she'd take her business card and if she could work on her behalf. Mindimooye took the card.

Months later, Mindimooye was sitting on the itchy wool pull-out in the basement when she got the call. She remembered trembling when the cordless rang cuz she just knew. And then her chest started pounding really fast cuz on the line was Alice, who told Mindimooye that she'd found her brother. My uncle Anthony. Anthony had also begun looking for his sister but got the year of her birth wrong.

Mindimooye didn't really reply. She just started doing a happy dance. A dance for each and every one of those years she didn't know anything.

That weekend she wrote an eager email to Alice that included the details she knew about her birth and listed her interests in "camping, hiking, running, biking, history, and photography." The next day, Alice forwarded the email from my uncle Anthony, which suggested he was raised by their birth mother. She read it closely, especially the part where he says her birth mother's name is Margaret Rose. Not was. Is.

At the same time, Mindimooye had kept up her search with another administrator at the public registry, who'd discovered another brother, Darrin. She shared my uncle Darrin's number with Mindimooye, and she called him.

Darrin was the first of the birth family we met that year. He wanted to meet Mindimooye right away, and he came up and stayed for the weekend following the call. As soon as they got off the phone, they got ready. It just seemed like the right thing to do.

Uncle Darrin drove from Toronto all the way north to Happyland in little over an hour. Mindimooye waited for him to arrive but didn't know what to do. She stepped out onto the porch and was waiting there when Darrin's car pulled into the driveway. He launched out of the driver's seat and ran to Mindimooye with a huge grin on his face. "Seeestor!"

They hugged, and then Uncle Darrin lurched his head back to get a good look at her.

"My GOD, you are so beautiful," he said. "I can't believe I have a seestor!"

Uncle Darrin showed Mindimooye baby pictures of them two, pictures of Nana Maggie. He promised he'd take Mindimooye to Fairford, Manitoba, to show her where they came from. While the heartbeat was still out, they began brainstorming how things would change and how they'd become a part of each other's lives from here on in.

I was too shy to come out and meet Uncle Darrin at first. I stayed in my room, lining up toy dinosaurs in a neat arrangement, something I'd done since I could crawl. Eventually O Touro called me into the living room, and there he was, with his leather jacket, thick and loose shag, and dirty blue jeans. His voice boomed through the house, and he shrieked and hollered at whatever joke he told or was told. I could tell we were related from the laugh alone.

A plan was made: Mindimooye, Anthony, Darrin, and Nana Maggie. A ten-day stay that spring.

O Touro and Mindimooye went to the airport to pick up Nana Maggie, who flew in from Black Canyon City, Arizona. Mindimooye waited at the drop-off with a bouquet, and around the corner she came.

Nana Maggie looked just like Mindimooye, and even like us three kids. Together in the living room, my siblings all looked at photos of nookomis, and Mindimooye would hold them up next to her own face, remarking at the similarity.

The fancy manicure alone was hard to forget. Total eye-pluckers painted tenderloin red. Ginormous rings on each finger. Gold pendant. Corona-bobbled earrings. In my most vivid brain pic of her, she's wearing a red turtleneck under a black vest and black harem pants embroidered with little flowery petals that alternated yellow and orange.

Nana Maggie had brought us gifts from Black Canyon City, including scorpions encased in domes of amber dew for me and Julian. And even though my sister was happy, she also felt sad for Nana Flo and for comparing the nanas to one another, what Mindimooye most feared. Nana Flo wasn't anything fancy, wasn't trying to impress anyone. But now here was Nana Maggie, the most done up of us all, carefully primped and covered in baubles. On one of the first nights, Nana Maggie and Kristine sat out together on the backyard porch and Maggie showed each ring on her finger and told her that "one day, these will all be yours."

Uncle Anthony drove in all the way from Fairford, bringing the rez with him. I remember him in the kitchen, giving us kids dream-catcher classes, his arms expanding to present the magnificent spreads of tradition he could fit in his suitcase and car to show his sis and us three. At some point during the trip Mindimooye went up to him and said, "You need to teach me how to be an Indian."

Uncle Anthony didn't say anything at first. It took him days to answer. Then right before he left to go back to Manitoba, he turned to Mindimooye and said, "I can't teach you how to be Indian, sis." He paused. "I can't teach you cuz you already are."

"Your Sister's on the Radio, Eh?"

About a month after Nana Maggie left, Kristine ran away. I found out from the bus driver. That's what she said one day before dropping me off at home.

Mindimooye didn't sleep for days. She couldn't eat. Right away she called the cops. Investigators went into the forests to look for her, scoured Happyland with Dutch and German shepherds. Everyone showed up to help look. But when they talked, Mindimooye couldn't hear them. The shock and hopelessness of the moment snapped something inside her. I found her smoking out back in the morning light early one day, the light in Kristine's room on and her drawers open for clues. The cops put Kristine's name on the radio and on TV and on the computer. Everywhere.

O Touro and Mindimooye weren't doing well, and Kristine had begun sneaking around at night with a boy they banned her from seeing, climbing out of her little basement room window.

One night they left and took off to the beach at the end of Soules Road, right beside Lake Couchiching. It was all fine until what looked like Mindimooye and O Touro's car pulled up and the headlights spotlit them. So they ran up Big Chief Hill and down the highway, worried they'd finally been caught. When they arrived at the Gordon Lightfoot Trail, an eleven-kilometre strip of gravel, asphalt, and boardwalk that runs along the lake, the car appeared again. They spent the night running and made it to a friend's house in Sunshine City, where Kristine had her very first shot of vodka.

I didn't know until much later, but Kristine ran away cuz she was scared the buckle would come for O Touro again, and that he'd hurt her like he did that one night in sixth grade when she stayed out past dark with a friend. Kicked her in the ribs with his construction boots. The kick left her in aftershock, and she stayed in bed for a week, watching the heartbeat rise and fall through the little basement window. O Touro made up for it with a blue Walkman.

But when Kristine came back home, she had had enough. She began yelling back at Mindimooye and O Touro, louder than they did. Her words would protect her no matter how vile they got. She transformed from scared little kid into adolescent rebel. No longer afraid, she knew that if O Touro ever touched her again she could and would peace out. She vented to Mindimooye about everything that was bothering her. She didn't want to get yelled at anymore. She didn't want to clean up after and take care of me and Julian anymore. And she didn't want O Touro in the house anymore.

Aanjigiboodiyegwaazone

Mindimooye and O Touro split up in July of 2002, shortly after Little Miss Dominion's birthday. It started slow. Earlier that year, O Touro slept through my seventh birthday party, and Mindimooye had to prep everything on her own. I remember her standing on her tippy-toes on a ladder to hang crepe-paper streamers from the living room ceiling fan, matching my Spider-Man birthday cake with Spider-Man napkins. Another day he picked her up from work and there was a cigarette with lipstick on it in the truck's ashtray. Then he disappeared for four days. It wasn't the first time he upped and left, but it happened just the same.

The day he came back to the house in Happyland, Julian and Mindimooye were in her bedroom, cuddling and watching a movie. O Touro walked in and told them he'd fallen in love with someone else, a dancer at the Elmvale strip club, and then off he went again.

Once he was gone and out the door, my brother sighed and swore in front of Mindimooye for the first time. "God, I hate him. He's such a fucking asshole." It was hard to argue otherwise.

Initially, Mindimooye was devastated. Her doctor suggested she take a week off work. She looked so low and depressed, and had sacrificed her own well-being and any budget from the PST booster pack and savings to cover the expenses of the house, which began to pile up, pipe after rotting pipe.

Kristine got a job at a local resort and took what money she had to give Mindimooye a fresh start, to cheer her up and make her feel nice. They went to Walmart, and Kristine led her through the aisles of the women's section, picking options off the racks. After a few minutes, Mindimooye stopped the cart and looked at my sister, tears welling in her eyes. "If you do this to me, I won't ever be the same ever again," she said. And then she wasn't.

After the Walmart trip, Mindimooye's mood shifted. In one of her journals from that time she describes "the refrigerator" lifting from her back and how she sought to change after what felt like a lifetime of holding her breath. She started to take care of herself. Take time for herself. Learned how to breathe all over again. Began to eat right. Began exercising every day. Began waking up at seven in the morning. She spent careful time practising her new signature, with her new name. She took up whole pieces of paper trying out that signature until she found something that felt right.

In July us four went on a vacation to Blue Mountain, and Mindimooye made the lavish suggestion that we try to get away once a season, even if only for a weekend. In September, she sent us back to school with brand-new Buffalo pencil cases and other supplies, and we spent the night before preparing our notebooks and ripping plastic from plastic.

We all hung around together more, going to the YMCA and the Cinema Four downtown and blowing through dozens of movies on DVD. Even Kristine dropped her surly tenth-grade ways with O Touro out of the house. She and Mindimooye would go out for manicures and tanning at the nail salon, or to the spa. We still fought sometimes, but for the most part things were peaceful. Even when O Touro showed up to grab me or Julian for a weekend visit, he gave off the impression of a more responsible and happier man. Tried to get back with Mindimooye once more, but this time she said no. He told Uncle Rob, "Figures now that she's not with me, she makes herself look gorgeous!"

By the new school year, Mindimooye had been training for three to four months and had dropped thirty pounds. Before, she hated the way she looked. But now she felt good, a thirty-eight-year-old single mother of three who'd dropped nearly ten dress sizes. New stomach, leg, and arm muscles. She was addicted and working toward summer 2003. Hopeful in time that she might find someone else, but for now liked her time with us. And we did too.

Graveyard Shift

The new Mindi brought me to Casino Rama for a scheduled tour. I was too young to go through the clockless game floor, a constipated place that never stopped blinking and ch-chinging and making or taking away the fortunes of countless hopefuls, aazha na gi-bookoshkaa? Instead, us two walked in through the hotel entrance to the foyer coliseum, where guests had gathered for the tour.

Supporting the coliseum stood tall pillars that spread around a medicine wheel engraved into the floor that also bore the grandfather teachings. Up close, the pillars felt and looked like maple bark, and high above displayed the carved busts of the grandfathers. There was a corresponding animal crest for each respective doodem. When she discovered who she was, who we were, Mindi told us we belonged to the Waabzheshi doodem, whom the casino interpreted as embodying "acceptance and generosity" and was responsible for "strategic planning and economic development." But with time I learned we belonged to another clan entirely.

Mindi loved working at the casino, and she was also quite good at it. In the span of a year she scored three promotions. It was the third one—to Senior Beverage Shift Supervisor—that us three kids collectively dubbed "The Promotion." We were thrilled. In brain pics, I saw us well on our way to millionaire status. The only problem was that Mindi went back on graveyard shifts.

The graveyard shift meant starting late and finishing before I was supposed to get up and ready for school. Everything was supposed to change when Mindi got that promotion, but the only thing that changed was the time she spent at home. She'd sleep all day until she had to go to work. We slimmed the cupboards down, but that had as much to do with the health-food kick Mindi went on around the time of The Promotion. We went from a Wonder Bread household to a Dimpflmeier one within those initial grocery hauls, and Mindi began making bowl after bowl of cottage cheese with bitter-ass grapefruit. Reeking salmon that she'd serve cold. What familiar staples she did buy, we ate quickly.

One night in the winter when she was on a graveyard shift, Kristine threw a house party and banished me and Julian and our red-headed and freckle-faced cousin Sanyo to Mindi's bedroom. For over an hour Julian and Sanyo tried to plot ways to get out while the bass boom of "Forgot About Dre" and other bops from the era rumbled the house floor silly.

When we finally got out, the house had filled up with kids drinking and hanging from the walls. Total *Jumanji*. I felt a chill coming from the bottom of the stairs, where the front door hung off the hinges thanks to um tolo. Julian and Cousin Sanyo took off to explore, seizing their McLovin moment to experience a real high school party. I made my way through the overcrowd and ended up in Julian's room, where some of the dweebier attendees took turns playing *Twisted Metal: Black* on his PlayStation One Mini. I found a spot to sit on the bottom bunk and tried to blend in next to a six-foot drunk kid who ended up freaking the hell out of me after he joked that his adam's apple would burst from his throat if I provoked it. An hour or two later he swept me up off my feet and held me by an ankle over the balcony railing, blood rushing to my dome. Someone passed out in a ditch. Someone stole a bunch of our DVDs. Someone broke a chair. And Kristine spent most of the night trying to fix the door.

Mindi wasn't too happy. The cops called her at work cuz Caillou's parents made a noise complaint. She had to leave work early, which got her in trouble with the shift manager. She never liked the thought of leaving us alone in the first place.

It was after this party that I moved on from lining up my dinosaurs and began to organize the remotes into neat lines and developed an eye for what could be made even, feeling strongly that even was better than odd.

Seventeen Years

One day in the summer of 2003 I found Mindi dancing around the kitchen island, sliding across the ceramic floor, stomping in and out of the light spots, smacking the cabinets and counters, and woo-hooing like I'd never heard any half-bad woo-hoo before. She kept shaking the divorce papers around in her hand like she'd won Lotto 6/49, screaming "Seventeen years! Seventeen years!" It was the relief that shocked me.

Chiclets

Mindi began seeing Hyde first. A shy, bashful neechie who worked at Casino Rama. Joked over the phone that she had to "try one of her own out." Never mind that the news had perked the ears of the many tipi crawlers who worked at the casino.

But Mindi told me she didn't feel like she deserved a second chance and felt shameful about dating again. Maybe she was just trying to keep her new life separate from her old one. When she did bring Hyde to the house she hid him in her bedroom. Not from us but us from him. Either way, it was clear: she did not want us all in the same brain pic.

Hyde and Mindi had been together for at least six months when they went into downtown Sunshine City for lunch at The Zoo, where they spotted their friend Candy on the patio day-drinking with Chiclets. Hyde and Mindi joined them, and a few beers and pricey burgers later Chiclets invited them over for dinner at his place, tucked at the end of Bass Lake Lane. Cobblestone Cottage.

Like always, dinner turned into a party. Candy did a bunch of coke, and Mindi hung out down at the dock, all by herself, always happy by the lake. At some point Hyde told Chiclets he'd take him to the city to meet "all kinds of chicks." When Mindi heard about that she was plenty pissed.

That night Chiclets said to her, "Tell you what: since that man doesn't know how to treat you well, I'd like you to take my card. Give me a call."

But Mindi didn't bother calling him cuz she isn't a cheater. Not even on Hyde. Until she realized she hadn't seen her purse in a couple days. Couldn't find it anywhere. She must have left it at Cobblestone Cottage. Left Chiclets' card in it. Left all the money for food in it.

But by miracle, Chiclets called the house phone.

"I got your purse. What's the schedule?"

"Just going to run 10k at the Y."

Chiclets bought a day pass and a brand-new spandex Under Armour wetsuit and spent his sweat session on a treadmill. After they finished, he handed Mindi her purse, and popped it: "Let me make you dinner."

When Mindi showed up at Cobblestone Cottage the second time, Chiclets had hors d'oeuvres laid out on the kitchen table and a vase of fresh stinkers handpicked from the perimeter of the property and now how about that. He fretted about what to cook and had asked around the office, went with a penne alla vodka.

Over dinner they talked about world events, even politics. For Mindi, this was next level. Back home it was just us three unworldly kids to talk with, and a house that was falling apart cuz O Touro stopped paying child support. Chiclets was kindness, fresh flowers. He was her age. Never been married. No kids. Tall, too.

Soon after that, Mindi stopped bringing Kristine to the salon or going shopping with her at the Sunshine City Square Mall. They quit sharing the tanning minutes and going to the Y together. They began fighting again. And then Mindi kicked her out of the house, just shy of her sixteenth birthday. Kristine was lying on the couch talking on the cordless when Mindi asked her to help out with the laundry, which we couldn't do at the house after the washer broke. Kristine told her fuck off, and that was that.

She began sleeping at her best friend's place in downtown Sunshine City. They stayed up late and went to parties on school nights. Mindi began going out more with her friends, too.

After two months, Mindi called Kristine's cellphone and told her she needed to talk. Asked to meet on the Lightfoot Trail. Kristine's friend and her mother lived off the trail, and my sister got her shoes on and went. Mindi had received some bad news from the doctor about her busy heart that week, and when Kristine found her on the trail in her tight jogging gear she was looking for forgiveness. She didn't know how long she'd be around. Kristine wonders if this was some loophole so that she didn't have to apologize for kicking her out but also so that she could keep on living the good life.

That night, Kristine's friend threw a party. Since everything felt end-of-the-worldish, my sister said fuck it, chugged some Canadian Club, and snorted her first line. After turning into a seasoned partier by the summer's end, she hit a bong on a weekend ecstasy binge. The combo rocked her the wrong way, and she ran out of the garage and onto the lawn, staring up at the dark sky. She looked so looney-tuned when her friends found her that they dropped her off at the house in Happyland. She burst through the door after months of being away, and as soon as Kristine saw the foyer light, she dropped to her knees. She lost control and watched in horror as her own body jerked and spasmed, screaming and wishing she could stop as Julian and I watched and wondered if this would go on forever.

Mindi called an ambulance, and they drove her to Soldiers' Memorial Hospital downtown. It took Kristine ending up in the ER for Mindi to ask her to come home. She came back that week but nonetheless continued to party. Mindi did too.

Big Chief Island

Not many locals know that Sunshine City was built on a graveyard. There are reports of workers and Mary Street homeowners finding bodies after digging up their basement floors. Dozens of remains from the days of intertribal warfare and secret villages. Accidental exhumations were common back then. Forceful grave robberies by locals and tourists even more so. In the twentieth century, some bodies were brought to Rama's chief at the time, who took them over to Big Chief Island.

Big Chief Island is about a fifteen-minute speedboat trip from the waterfront, ten if in a hurry to snag a good spot. Unfortunately for the dead buried there, since the 1970s the inlet has had a party reputation among butterfly towns in Simcoe County and beyond. It remains largely unoccupied until the summer months, when it mutates into a saggy and sunburnt rodeo that some call Golden Pond. Then it's time to get tipsy, piss in the lake, toss a beer in the water, and have fun. Nobody swims when they go to Big Chief. The water never goes past the waist anyways.

Story goes, Mindi's first boater party at Big Chief Island with the good-lifers turned into a four-day trip. They went out on Chiclets' friend's boat, *Cooper's Crib*, named after his baby boy. Rows and rows of boats hooked up to one another, with dinghies rigged to jumping platforms waiting for a spin. They were always drinking and getting a bit too blitzed off Coronas on houseboats named after their kids or businesses.

Chiclets brought a camera and got people to take pictures of them all, of him and Mindi especially. Them two look happy in those photos. Anything looks happy next to those Chiclets. It seemed as if they'd known each other from another life. Truth is, Chiclets clung to Mindi instantly. Right away began telling everybody she was his girlfriend. Introduced her to his big-ass family before us three ever met him. There was no conversing about it, even though she'd met him only a few times before. But lots of bells and whistles and limos and parties changed that. Relax, put those feet up. It was only Mindi's first time out, and the girls were already painting her toes on the bow of the boat.

Some of the girls were Mindi's age but most were a little younger. The guys were all Sunshine City kids who went way back. Chiclets grew up with what Mindi called "old money," and so did Cooper's O Touro and uncle, who also had boats, along with their friends, who also had boats, enough to fill an entire row on their own. These bigwig daddies hailed from the Family Compact, old head proprietors who owned funeral homes and manufacturing facilities that produced equipment for gold milling in the Dakotas.

The day Chiclets came to pick her up, Julian and I were about to unlock Gold Sonic on Sega Genesis. Neither of us noticed Mindi packing more than normal.

I hated playing Tails. Tails was bottom bunk. He couldn't fit in the screen if Sonic took off. And boy did Sonic like to take off. Lo, one is destined to fall behind frame with a name like Tails. And Tails lost us more coins than he was worth, so we decided to let Julian get Gold Sonic on his own. I sat on the bed and watched on. It was then we heard the front door open, followed up with a hellooooo from Mindi running up the stairs. I watched her walk back and forth through the frame of the bedroom door.

I went out into the hallway and saw Chiclets at the bottom of the stairs. "Where's my mom?"

"Just in here, babe," Mindi called out from the bedroom. Said she only came to grab a few things, pack a bag or two for the night.

"Where you going?"

"Out. Just for the night, babe. Back tomorrow."

I turned around for Julian's reaction but only got a view of his slouched back. He just kept staring at the screen, collecting rings. And then Mindi gave me a kiss and went out the front door. And it wasn't until a few months or so later that us three realized them two had no plans to come back to Happyland anytime soon.

The Kris Who Stole Christmas

That summer when Mindi was off good-lifing with her boater pals, O Touro would come every other weekend (and eventually every other other weekend) to pick Julian and me up and bring us to his townhouse on the river near Wasaga Beach, where we'd meet his buddies and new girlfriends. At the house in Happyland, Kris started playing "In da Club" as loud and long as she possibly could without blowing the speakers, cuz there were no adults around to stop her.

Then came Muchachi. Muchachi was Kris's boyfriend and the first holy shit rich person I'd ever met. A well-connected dope dealer who sold tons and tons of weed and grew up rich to begin with and worked for cops and other high-ups like the mayor of a nearby butterfly town. There was nobody stopping him. Nobody to bring him to heel. Except Kris.

Kris and her friends loved making fun of Muchachi: his noughties guido look, bootcut jeanage, booth tan, pimply skin, too-pretty ways, how he took an hour to beat his face in the bathroom. His braces. The distortion of his ego and the transparency of his money. How he took Kris to the Cinema Four in a limo. Like, who does that? Even I played jokes on Muchachi, hiding his busy clamshell flip-phone when he wasn't looking. But Kris stayed with him cuz it helped fill the fridge, and when he drove her to class at Patrick Fogarty he'd pour a wad of Bordens and Lyon-Kings into her purse.

When he showed up to the house and brought an Xbox with him, I watched him and Kris and Julian take runs shooting zombies that endlessly charged at them, Usher's heavy breathing heavy blasting on the surround sound. Muchachi paid little heed to my age, speaking to me more seriously than he did with his little brother, who was also eight, though he could see I got embarrassed if grown-up topics like sex came up.

"Hey, Cody."

"Yeah, Muchachi?"

"I bet I can make you say *sex*."

"No way."

"Wanna bet? Say *ex* ten times fast."

"Ex ex ex ex exsexsexsex . . . that's cheating!"

Over the course of that fall, Muchachi and Kris would fight every couple days, stupid and petty and over-the-top arguments, yet somehow Kris always had the higher ground. One night I was listening to them volley screams downstairs while I pretended to sleep on one of the green leather couches, which I'd migrated to and semi-regularly wet after Mindi left. Eventually, Muchachi took off in dramatic, soap opera tears. After he drove off, I went to Kris's room and sat with her on her bed. We watched as he called her cellphone again and again. When she finally picked up, I could hear him blubbering dumbly about the nature of his soul, begging for her love. He crashed into roadside bushes on his way back to his parents' mansion twenty minutes from the Eastside of Happyland.

"Tell me not to kill myself. Please, baby. I love you! I fucking LOVE you. You're the only girl I need!"

She whispered for me to answer, and then I did: "Please don't kill yourself, Muchachi."

"Is that you, little Code? So good to hear your voice, bro!"

In the end, Kris forgave him, like she always did. Muchachi came back to the house, and we watched another Blockbuster DVD.

When Kris wasn't getting money from Muchachi, she got resourceful in other ways, like stealing groceries from the local A&P. She took me to the children's clothing store in the Sunshine City Square Mall and into the fitting room with her, where she tried on a coat and stuffed clothes into her backpack and underneath the ones she was already wearing.

"What are you doing?"

"Just trying it on. Shh."

"Why's it in your bag then?"

She shushed me again. "Paid in advance. Remember, Code?"

Paid in advance. Fooled me.

When winter rolled around, Mindi asked Kris to work the door at the annual casino staff holiday party at Tux II, Sunshine City's only "club." It was a peace offering for taking off and leaving us three on our own. Easy money. Not to mention Kris still hadn't forgiven Mindi for kicking her out, but she was willing to accept any opportunity to spend time with her. Plus what teenager doesn't like working the door? She walked in with a plan, pocketing every other twenty-dollar ticket sold to put toward the Christmas fund. Ended up stealing around five hundred dollars, and then they paid her on top of that. Mindi got tipsy and didn't notice anyways.

A few days later, Kris and Muchachi drove to Home Depot and paid in advance for a Christmas tree. She paid in advance for the tinsel, the spray-on frost, the white and icy-blue decorations, even the angel. The tree looked freezing and warm at the same time.

When Mindi and Chiclets arrived from Cobblestone Cottage after months of living the good life, Mindi was wearing Kris's fluffy white turtleneck, her hair straightened and forked. They took pictures together on the couch, backdropped by the frozen tree. Kris had filled the entire perimeter of the tree base with paid-in-advance gifts and passed us present after present that she'd wrapped in gold and silver tissue and paper that glistened and sparkled under the string lights.

Kris was pissed that Mindi played it off in front of Chiclets like she was the one who froze the tree, who bought the presents for Julian and me. She was pissed that Mindi took her paid-in-advance regalia for her dates with Chiclets. Never during that trip to Walmart did Kris think Mindi would go from that dishevelled flower into full noughties baddie. But Mindi had to look good for her own limos.

The Pipes

After their Christmas visit, Mindi and Chiclets left again, and the layers of the house in Happyland began to pull apart one by one. Starting with the pipes, which were doomed to begin with and now approaching the end of their life. Made of copper that couldn't withstand the endless sulphur and was breaking down trying to convey it all.

The rot was preventable. But cuz the house was built on a swamp—which Mindi had discovered one day when she mowed the backyard and families of crayfish poured out, scrambling for life—it had drawn in water high in sulphur. The sulphur made the taps stink like pizza farts and caused premature corrosion and leaky pipes. The right thing to have done as soon as the first pipe rusted was to install more osmosis systems to make the water potable. Maybe an iron-filter softener system could have solved replacing the pipes. Or we could have shocked the well every month or so to regenerate it. Or if O Touro hadn't racked up so much debt under Mindi's name, they could have taken a loan out to replace the copper with PEX. But what happened instead, before the two of them left, was that they would pay a few hundred to fix one, and then another one would burst.

To get to the top bunk in Julian's bedroom meant having to walk across his broadloom stained by leaks and mould, the filch of it squishing under our feet. So much water had seeped into the bedroom that a rank dampness began to emanate from his walls and ooze out into the hallway. The dampness sucked on our skin. And it stunk like a bunch of dead fish sitting in wet dog.

Kris dropped out from Patrick Fogarty, and Julian and I began missing a lot of days at Notre Dame Catholic, with our attendance petering off after New Year's. We rarely caught the bus, which drove off right as we cracked open the front door, Caillou waving goodbye from his window seat. When I did manage to catch it, I'd try to get some sleep as my noggin rested against the window vibrating from the unpaved backroads.

That year there were multiple lice outbreaks, and I think us three caused at least one. Mindi came home from Cobblestone Cottage and put a hot bag on my head that burned as she combed through and picked for eggs. When she was gone again, Bear got fleas, and then we did too. We ended up with bites that took forever to go away and itched the more we scratched.

At Notre Dame, I could slim into the gym and reliably find the breakfast club's saran-wrapped blueberry muffins and raisin bagels just before class began. But when lunchtime came, I usually had only a pack of sesame snaps or a piece of fruit that soiled the bottom of my bag. A kind teacher or two sometimes took me aside and gave me lunch.

Kris got inventive with stretching food across the weeks. Sometimes it was Kraft Dinner with too much ketchup. Sometimes I'd snack on brittle, fudge, and candies from Muchachi. Sometimes it was a Kraft cheese slice. Sometimes it was Domino's. And sometimes it was nothing. One weekend I fell asleep in the living room starving my mouth off. I woke up hungry and stood up, but couldn't make it to the kitchen and passed out on a chair in the dining room, hoping for someone to come get me.

We were dehydrated. E. coli breached the taps, plus our water wasn't heated and we couldn't pay in advance for those heavy blue jugs Mindi used to buy for the Culligan cooler. So we began boiling water to drink. Mindi had taught us that clear piss was better than yellow piss, but we were all yellow piss. The fountains of Notre Dame became one of the main water sources, and I used to put my lips directly on the taps cuz I didn't know any better.

In the spring we plugged our noses and ventured into Julian's room to move his TV and video games upstairs.

Once inside, I asked Julian to show me what mould was. He pointed to the bluish-purple fluffs blooming in and around his television stand. It had been growing, but slowly, over months. Our feet were soggy from his discoloured and wet carpet. A hundred pens had leaked.

He led me to his closet, pulled back the sliding door, and showed me how the wall dividing it from the laundry room had rotted to a pulp and begun eating the beams and guts. We could see the contractor's stamp on the wood.

The sulphur killed the houseplants, except for one adult cactus and a tree that was older than me. We started boiling water on the stove for baths, before we stopped taking baths.

Then the lights went out.

44°40'21.6"N 79°24'23.0"W

Time slowed down without Mindi or O Touro. With neither of them around to animate things, the rooms dusted up and got stale. Their absence yoked us three to keep the house and what happened inside it top secret from the schools and neighbours.

One of the immediate perks to having no grown-ups living with us was that I no longer needed permission to eat a whole package of El Paso soft tacos or a box of cereal in one go. Nobody got mad at me if I took finger swabs of salted butter and slices of Wonder Bread. Mayonnaise sandwiches. Couldn't keep my hands out the pickle jar. We emptied the fridge and pantry and the cupboards until what remained was whatever Mindi jarred and dated years before, much of it huddling in the fridge corners, left to expire long ago.

We played slugs, zipping ourselves into sleeping bags upside down and worming along the floor in the dark to find one another and pounce. There were epic fights over internet time. Kris wanted to email her friends and crushes, and Julian wanted to play *Warcraft III: Reign of Chaos* and flash games. Kris blamed Julian for the viruses that started popping up on the computer and hid the keyboard under The Plasma.

Burdocks started to pop up in the garden: the fewer people in the house there were, the more burrs grew. The burdock spread from the garden and into patches alongside the house's perimeter, settling fights between yarrow and mugwort for space along the sides. It weeded out any natural flowers growing around it, cuz burdocks are a dominant species and weeds are just lived-in flowers showing up where they can and taking what they need to make it to the next day. Nothing wrong with that.

Our cousins Sanyo and Leeroy came over for endless tournaments of *Super Smash Bros. Melee* and evening wars against the neighbourhood kids who were talking shit about us and the house, smearing us like another foot full of Bear's dog crap on the carpet. I played entire co-op campaigns of *Baldur's Gate: Dark Alliance II* wide-eyed at four in the morning with Julian, and one night alone found the Flood in *Halo*, the crunch of those slightly sweet, slightly salty No Name soda wafers.

One day, Julian and a kid from up the street started building a treehouse in the front. They made steps to the top and a crawlway out of old fence posts and nails from O Touro's shed that bled orange after a spring storm came through the Eastside of Happyland. They found leftover sheets of plywood and nailed them to branches, enough pieces to develop a plankway or two and a bucket pulley system that carried our newest kitties from Uncle Rob to the highest level.

We were playing in the treehouse one day when O Touro showed up in a new truck, fresh from another treatment centre, and tore the whole thing down. Told us we needed something proper. He bought a bunch of wood from Home Depot, began with the legs at the base, and then put up three walls. And then he left again. Never finished it. Telling you.

Mr. Sour Cream and Onion

Like many half-bads before me, I sat at the edge of the driveway in the dead of July with Pokémon cards in one hand. The heartbeat hung low behind Caillou's bungalow and stained all of Eastside a nosebleed red. Dirt covered both knees from playing in the forest. Another hot one. Rash on the crotch, dry mouth, water-craving hot.

I was shuffling through the Pokémon cards, keeping the rare shiny ones from Julian in the middle of the deck and the normies at the front and rear. My fingers flipped through and flicked whatever bits of sand or dirt away. Like Julian, I didn't know how to play the game. I just liked the holographic pictures, stats, and attack descriptions.

Two kids approached me. I didn't know their names, but I knew they lived at a still-renovating house up the road that we passed on our trips to the corner store. They had a decent trampoline and sometimes invited the neighbourhood kids over to bounce and scream. They wore cargo shorts and sports hats and running shoes that fit.

"How many cards you got?" the older kid asked.

"A few good ones. Lotta basics, like Nidorino, Bulbasaur, Chikorita . . ." I trailed off, noticing the can of sour cream and onion Pringles tucked in his armpit like a football. The moustache man on the green tube stared at me, thin brows curved over pencil-dot eyes. Hi, Code Monster. It's me, Mr. Sour Cream and Onion. My dry mouth flooded with saliva.

They saw me staring and grinned.

"How about a trade?"

"What you have to trade?" I asked, scanning them for a deck of cards.

The kid shook the can.

Back inside, I was slouched in front of the television in the middle of the messiest of bedrooms, next to the now excavated can of Pringles, pulling hair to *The Legend of Dragoon*. I was stuck on the fourth disc, in the infamous City of Law, and had been for a while. Julian had promised to help if I gave him the stolen fund-raiser Toblerone I'd been saving till school ended. But after he ate it, he confessed he didn't know how to leave either.

Kris shouted that Domino's had arrived, and I followed her to the dining room, where Muchachi and his little brother sat with their hands on the table before the flyer-special pizza. Julian was spending another weekend at a friend's place and Kris was flipping out over unpaid bills. Mindi would pay one here and there, but we never knew what we were losing until it was gone. Each month brought new surprises: satellite, internet, and the phone line. We probably lost heat but thankfully didn't need it.

"What's this say?" Muchachi's little brother asked, pointing at the pizza box. Even though he was nine like me, the little brother couldn't read well.

"'Total satisfaction guaranteed,'" I said. Like Domino himself just knew we'd love it.

Kris opened the first box. Canned heat waves steamed our faces, and we immediately began tearing slices away and ripping the dipping sauce open before it could expire on us. We giggled and told jokes with our mouths full of sauce and cheese and pepperoni and talked about how good it tasted. After the first two slices, Kris told me to grab plates.

I went into the kitchen, opened the dishwasher that stopped working mid-wash, and stacked the plates on the island. I opened the fridge and saw a lonely pickle, takeout ketchup packets, and an unfinished bottle of Clamato juice that had gone off. The pale fridge light broke across the kitchen and spotlit Bear's empty dog bowl in the corner.

I slammed the fridge shut and went back into the dining room with the plates. We ate the rest of the pizza.

Jarsick

Deep into summer, the yard was nothing but a bunch of dry, burnt plants wherever the weeds didn't grow. Then the weeds grew over the dead stuff and over the well. From the front of the yard to the side and the back, pricks tickled any exposed bits, and Bear covered the carpets with burrs that clumped together his golden fur. The flowers in the garden didn't show up again, and for the second summer in a row we were the only ones with straw for grass on the Eastside of Happyland. I saw so on our walks to get groceries from the corner store down the highway.

Julian and I watched Kris dump out the insides of a jar onto O Touro and Mindi's bed. Mindi used the jar to collect tips from work and any change she found in the vacuum. A waterfall of red and silver copper chink-chinked until it covered a small corner of the blanket. Julian and Kris gathered the change and sorted it into bigger piles while I made smaller ones.

"Do you see any loonies?" Kris asked, pushing pennies out of the way only to find more blanket.

"I'm not going to the corner store with pennies again," Julian said.

"Want to eat or not? Take your brother with you, and get me tampons." We slipped our shoes on in the foyer. Kris came with us to the porch and sat on the stone with a lighter and a smoke in her hand. "Get some Wonder Bread, too!"

"What way we taking?" I asked.

"Same way."

We walked up the Eastside of Happyland and then down a backroad, following Highway 11, our pockets full of nickels. By the time our feet cramped up, there it was: a sunburnt shack bleached by the yard-killing heartbeat and two gas pumps for anybody heading north to Muskoka cottage country, where people have houses to take breaks from their houses. Blink after the chipped Santa's Village billboard below the Highway 11 overpass and you'll miss the turn entirely. If you're eating burgers, you're too far gone. All the ditches were dried out and shrivelling up. We always came back with a bag of Wonder Bread and a bag of Doritos. Nothing went mouldy except the basement walls.

One day I went out back and a brown puddle of sop soaked both shoes when I stepped off the deck onto the grass. From the deck to the line where the backyard met the forest, the yard our uncles and aunties and friends used to camp on had gone full swamp. The septic underneath the house had burst and cursed our toilets sick by having them puke up whatever little came out of us three. My footsteps squished along the bumpy ground until a caterpillar caught my eye. Squiggling along minding its own business. I went and got a mason jar, a fat one Mindi drank out of, and left it on the grass next to the caterpillar. He didn't go in. So I picked him up and plopped him gently in the jar. I threw in a leaf or two from the maw for good luck and then ripped up some fresh ones from the cedars lining our property. But even under a leaf pile, the caterpillar looked thirsty in the glass. Old calcified white spots from the dishwasher stopped him from climbing out. Made him carsick in the jar.

When it got dark out, I brought the jar into a room with a bulb that still worked. The caterpillar bobbed and pawed at the glass while I took an end piece from the bag of Wonder Bread and poked at the warts on my feet.

In the morning, I put the jar on its side and let the caterpillar out onto the deck and the tempered-glass patio table. I let him surf and put a finger in front of him when I wanted him to go somewhere else. Julian and I walked to the edge of the Eastside of Happyland and then probably down Highway 11 and down some backroads that went so far I could swear we were finally getting out of there, but only ended up on more Highway 11. Eventually we got tired of walking around and came back in the front door.

"Mom called."

"What did she say?"

"That she's on her way back."

Cousins Sanyo and Leeroy came over, banging pots and pans and dog-dancing with Bear to get a laugh out of us. We fired up the Xbox Muchachi left behind and played *Halo*. Julian and Sanyo told jokes that I was too young to understand but made me laugh anyways, just from the way they said them. Even though I was a little kid who never left them alone, they still gave me a chance to kick their butts on the biggest multiplayer map, a glassed-over and frozen war zone called Sidewinder. They liked *Halo* too much to ever let me win out of pity. But just when I was about to beat them, Julian began to complain about the light shining in his eyes from the dining room window.

The caterpillar went full cocoon shortly after that. I woke to a bed of webs on the side of the jar. I wanted to watch something grow in the house and fly out, something that would grow out the jar and along the living room walls like that bean project in first grade.

As the days got hotter, we spent our nights cooling down in Kris's room in the basement, despite its proximity to Julian's and the laundry room, both of which could kill us three easy-peasy back then. Began making one big room lemon squeezy. On the computer, Julian ripped from the web a single *Family Guy* episode, the one about the end of the world and all the Twinkies that came after. We watched it every night. Sometimes twice.

Then, when he wasn't stuck watching me, Julian began spending every minute he could at Sanyo and Leeroy's place. Getting lost in the forest connected to their backyard, snoozing in their basement with an overworked PlayStation 2 and a Great Dane named Sausage, and trips to a tall silver fridge filled with I don't even know what.

At the house in Happyland, Kris and I topped up Bear's metal bowl with the dregs of his dog food and tossed the empty bag beside a stack of pizza boxes. The cocoon held steady to the inside of the jar. Still waiting for the right time to butterfly.

Cottage Season

Mindi came back, but not for good. Took us on a blister-inducing walk along the backroads to Lake Simcoe and grabbed some things from the house to bring to Cobblestone Cottage. She'd officially moved in with Chiclets and we'd officially run out of ideas of what to eat.

What's worse, her constituents and manager knew what was happening with the medical leave she posted that summer, and that see-you-next-Tuesday of a supervisor finally succeeded in getting her canned from the casino as planned after spotting Mindi around Sunshine City. Casino Rama could fire you for unsatisfactory performance, dishonesty, insubordination, failure to maintain your gaming registration, or serious misconduct, and they didn't include any provisions for aanjigiboodiyegwaazone. The point of no return.

One afternoon Mindi didn't show up after saying she'd spend the day with us. Kris called her up and fought with her over the phone saying that a promise is a promise. When they hung up,

Cousin Leeroy drove Kris to Cobblestone Cottage in his new car and they parked out front.

From there, Mindi remembers them two coming into the house and screaming at her for Kris's stuff back and that Chiclets had no idea Mindi was supposed to be home. But Kris remembers finding them having a blast in the backyard, getting down on her knees and begging Mindi to come home, only for Mindi to refuse. So pick whichever iteration is more appealing, I guess.

Either way, Kris came home in tears, Cousin Leeroy consoling her. Mindi wasn't far behind, pulling up in Chiclets' Jeep in a rage, asking what the hell that was all about. Then the buckle came for Leeroy, who yelled at Mindi, look at what you're fucking doing to your kids. Then the buckle came for Mindi, who said something nasty about Leeroy's mother to his face, nasty enough to make Leeroy cry and slam the door on his way out. She turned to us and asked if we were happy now, though at the time we were anything but.

Mindi was gone again by the morning. Without a job, she had no choice but to give the house up. Whoever bought it only paid what remained on the mortgage and told us we could keep renting it from him after the title transferred.

O Touro called Mindi at Cobblestone Cottage a few days later and said he wanted to meet. Even though he was working for Hydro One, he toggled between the riverside townhouse and a treatment centre. After finishing treatment, he drove to Cobblestone Cottage and brought a piece a paper for Mindi to sign. Told her to take all the time she needed.

Mindi believed in the agreement, thought he'd take over the bills and move in again, and so she signed the paper. But O Touro was unable or unwilling to pay child support and by signing the paper, Mindi forgave the backpay, worth tens of thousands. He told Mindi he wanted to watch after us again, but again he left in the truck.

Practising

The day we were finally rescued I was playing with Caillou in his yard. His dad mowed the lawn every Saturday morning, making the uneven patches around our house stand out even more. Everything ugly and bulky got pushed to the edges of their property, except for Caillou's playhouse, which sat smack dab in the middle of the backyard by itself.

Caillou dropped his shorts to pee with me on the fence behind the playhouse. "What you think about sex, Cody?"

"What about it? We're too young for that stuff, aren't we?"

"Are you too young to swear? Then you're not too young for sex."

I pulled up my shorts. "My mom said I'm not allowed to swear. And I don't want to have sex."

"You better start practising cuz it's coming soon. You know that, don't you?"

"We have no wives to practise it with."

"Don't you want to be good at sex by the time you get married?"

"I don't know if I want to get married."

"C'mon. I practise with the guys up the road all the time. It's fine."

"Can't we just play in the forest again?" I asked.

Caillou clicked his tongue. "You're not gonna get any toys. Everybody in the neighbourhood knows you need new toys. You know what they've been saying about you?"

Caillou had been telling me about these toys for a couple days. Although Kris had paid in advance for a GameCube from Walmart, Mindi hadn't gotten me anything for my ninth birthday that year. Grudgingly, I followed him into the playhouse, laid down on the floor, and worried about splinters. Caillou told me to flip around and do as he did. I saw the missing skin at the tip of him and wondered if he'd tried to have sex with his dog. After a bit, I heard Julian coming toward the playhouse and calling for me. I pulled up my shorts and ran out the door.

"We gotta go," Julian said.

Just beyond him was a glossy white Infiniti in our gravel driveway. By the time we walked over, Auntie Meesh had stepped out of the car, yapping like she was taking us on vacation. She told us we had a half-hour to pack but that her kids had spares if needed.

I packed a bag, tossed it in the spacey trunk, and hopped in the back seat. The digitized dials on the dashboard glowed freezie red and beep-blooped. It was first bit of air-con I felt all summer. Julian squished in the back with me and closed the door. Then Auntie Meesh came in, followed by Kris in shotgun.

"This is it, guys. Brand-new Infiniti. Nice, eh? You're gonna love the drive."

Meesh pushed the start button, pumped the speakers up, and whooshed out of the driveway, and after we landed on the freeway I began to worry about Bear and the jarsick caterpillar, both of whom were left in the house. I tongued my cankers until they quit singing.

PART II

THE BULL

Improper

The heartbeat was coming down by the time Auntie Meesh chauffeured us three into the suburbs of Alliston and pulled up to her McMansion.

I didn't know it at the time, but that summer some of the faux aunties had stepped up to intervene. Called O Touro and told him to get his shit together. Auntie Meesh found out Mindi and O Touro had stopped living at the house and paying bills, so she decided to drive over and pick us three up.

"Welcome, babes! Your two-thousand-square-foot vacay officially begins now!"

Like many McMansions, Auntie Meesh's fibbed on sight: it was tight-squeeze and cookie-cutter and copy-kitten on the outside but doubled in size and electrified my insides once we stepped into the foyer and our shoes mixed into the family's mass of boots and sandals. One look was all it took to see that this place was determined to have its shit together. The first thing I noticed were the tiles, which I swear were the same in the kitchen as in the office and in the two living rooms. The second thing was a foyer staircase that wrapped around a chandelier of phony crystals with rainbows strewn to infinity and beyond. The third was a black-and-blue-tongued chow chow pup, aptly named Chow-Chow.

The McMansion had more than enough square feet to comfortably fit Auntie Meesh and her hubby, their five kids, and us three. Every bit of furniture was plush to the touch and looked conditioned with Vaseline, garnished with novelty pillows, throws, and plenty of Lego blocks and other doorstoppers. The rooms banked on Meesh's "contemporary" palette for textured paints: plum and piss and blood and puke. Total Ikea, circa early 2000s. The cognac stink of the place was heavy, like a secret: like something covering something up. (It wasn't until a week or two passed that I realized it was wet dog.) There was always a crowd of us gathering around a desktop or countertop or hot topic, partaking in some saucy conversation about the business of McMansion richness or local libel cases. Lots of giggling and wiggling and glittering gold flakes and taking for granted happening, but I was happy to spend time with people who looked like they knew something we didn't.

Best part of Meesh's house was the basement. The first time I'd visited, when I was four or five, the older boys led me into the pitch darkness of the closet, promising me treasure or candy, only to lock the door behind me and unleash the terrifying shrieks of a McMansion velociraptor. Now I appreciated the basement at my ripe age, took stock of the clutter under the couches and new brands of nutty chocolate and nougat and serial killers on the TV and unfinished plates of food that someone left under a table. They had a projector and a plasma-screen that burned your eyes like a theatre and games that Julian and I had never played before. Her older children watched pay-per-view all night, nonstop.

Most mornings I was the first person awake, finding everybody passed out in the basement couches, in one of the two living rooms, or on the floor. I could hear Meesh and her hubby snoring away in their bedroom. I'd wander around the McMansion and pet Chow-Chow and chew and slurp through as many bowls of cereal as possible before anyone else woke up and reminded me whose food it was.

At nighttime, Meesh sent me to bed with a pointed finger-snap. Go. No arguing. Eleven o'clock sharp every night. I was nine years old, and nobody had set me a bedtime in ages. Who did this auntie of mine think she was? I was closest in age to her youngest son, so naturally I got the same bedtime as him and slept on his floor. He snored as loud as she did. Louder than the zoo and lullaby tune tapes we fell asleep to. I'd be lying on the floor for hours, whimpering and getting teary-eyed to this tape that taught us how to count sheep. After a week or two, I told Meesh I couldn't fall asleep cuz the boy snored and Meesh came up and showed me how to replay the tape. I prayed every day she'd let me sleep in the basement with the TV painting our faces with horror or cartoon, maybe even a bag of Lay's or Doritos within reach.

We had to eat at the dinner table and with forks and knives and spoons. We already did that, but there was something about the way they had to remind us, like we wouldn't know to do it ourselves. Meesh and her hubby laughed at Julian for eating spaghetti wrong. One time the kid and I stayed up late playing *Grand Theft Auto:*

Vice City. He blew up a bunch of cops and strippers and grand-pops and cheat-coded himself a rocket launcher and an army tank. When he got hungry he paused the game, waddled upstairs, and came back with a bag of Lay's. I can still hear the squeak from the bag being opened. I was so hungry I was shaking. After a couple handfuls, the kid snatched the bag away and told me I was eating improperly.

"What you mean improperly?"

"You're taking handfuls. That's improper. Eat them one at a time. Like this." We took turns eating one salt-and-vinegar chip at a time, and I wanted to sock him until his nose bled. Once he passed out and started snoring, I grabbed handfuls and shoved them into my mouth until the bag was empty. I tossed it into the growing trash-and-toy mound in the corner of the basement.

One day about a month in, Kris left the McMansion in a hurry. O Touro had called Auntie Meesh to say that Mindi had picked up a bunch of furniture from the house in Happyland and put it away in a storage unit. Kris was shocked cuz Mindi told her she would leave the furniture for us three. So Meesh took Kris into town to meet Mindi at the storage unit, just as the heartbeat sank. Right away they could see Mindi was a bit tipsy, talking heavy shit and grabbing Kris's hands whenever she tried to take something out of the unit. They had their first-ever fist fight, while Meesh watched on. Punches were thrown and hair got pulled and Kris's foot slid on broken glass and bled everywhere before Meesh finally broke them up.

After the fight, Kris went back to the house in Happyland, which was filthy and almost empty. She laid on the piss-whiff couch, staring at the ceiling fan, oscillating between wanting to kill herself and trying to fix things. She made a decision that night that would change things for us all.

At the beginning of August, O Touro came to pick me up in his truck. As I packed a bag I saw that Julian stayed sitting on his bed. He'd gotten his own room at Auntie Meesh's, even scored a gig as a dishwasher. I have a brain pic of him cashing his first paycheque at the Trust and the smile on his face when he did it.

"Are you coming?"

"No."

"Why not?"

He just shook his head and looked down at the floor. O Touro was outside waiting for me, so I left the room, said goodbye to whoever was around at the time, hopped in the truck, and went to pick up Kris. Cuz the three of us were moving into a new place in Sunshine City, bud.

To this day I still can't count sheep, and I still eat chips by the handful.

Day the Pack Came

The next morning, I was chilling in the basement of the house in Happyland poking at my plantar warts. Painful craters of them chunked on my clammy feet. The heels and webs got particularly crowded, and one on my right heel got so deep from walking barefoot and sockless around Eastside that it gave me hobbit-foot.

O Touro bounced between rooms and through the hallways. "Pack up. Let's go. Pack up. C'mon, guys."

He came downstairs and found me hunched over, trying to pull a wart out with a butter knife. I was sitting next to a dried pool of nail polish that I'd tossed from the top floor balcony a couple months back. Just beyond this pool was some Bear shit that'd been sitting there for anywhere between five weeks and three months, smeared into the coarse matting that covered most of the sprawling basement floor.

"Didn't you hear me? Time to pack up and get moving, Cody. Telling you right now. Come help me."

I took a good look at him: clean-shaven from the neck up. Coughing lots. Likely an off-white Molson Canadian or otherwise novelty T-shirt that would go for dozens in deadstock or vintage stores today with some paint stains from a previous move and a cardboard box from the grocery store between his arm and his waist. The foyer light crowned his Bic'd head and formed a nimbus around his neck.

He and I scanned the floor together and like always he took the first step. "C'mon, bud. Help me clean this up. What happened in here? Can't get a step in, for Chrissake." Beyond the door were piles of laundry and VHS tapes in little towers, plus a floor full of old toys. One of the towers had crash-landed next to the television. I stepped over the synthesis of Lego sets and Mega Bloks spilt from an oversized bin and the scattered tapes before sitting beside the television. I began stacking video games into piles. "Julian's gonna want me to bring these."

O Touro handed me the grocery box. "And I'm telling you right now there's no way we're leaving that TV behind."

"How many truckloads you think we'll do?"

"However many the new place can take."

I went out to the porch and Kris sat with me on the bottom step with her head hung low, playing with the thong of her sandal. She hadn't slept much. "You're going first and I'm going with the next load."

I dug little holes into the gravel. "And when's Julian coming to get his things?"

"Don't know. Don't think he wants to switch schools again. Don't think he's coming back. Don't think he wants to quit his job. Don't think there's much for him to grab."

I watched O Touro and his bud fill the truck with the heavy items. I packed the PlayStation One Mini into my backpack and waited out front until they finished up. They brought The Plasma and the piss-whiff couches and the wood coffee table and then O Touro took the keys from his pocket for a jingle.

"Ready?"

"Think so."

"Get in then."

"Is Bear coming?"

"Can't have Bear at the new place," O Touro said. He lifted the ramp up and back into the truck. "No room. Your mother's taking him to the city."

"When's she coming to take him then?"

O Touro coughed the question off and locked the rear latch.

"And when's Julian coming back?"

"Get in the truck, son."

I hopped into shotgun. The belt felt warm against my arm and the buckle was hot to the touch when I clicked in. I waited for O Touro to finish speaking to Kris, who just kept shaking her head.

O Touro swore, coughed a bunch, lit a cig, shut his door, rolled down the windows, clicked in, revved the engine once or twice, and then shifted out of park and into drive. In the mirror I watched Kris walk back into the house to pack more small things. And then we turned the corner to join the rest of Highway 11.

I didn't realize then how much of our stuff we were leaving behind. More than half of it. Most of Julian's room had been sitting in mould for too long to salvage anything. A couple sofas and loveseats got left in the basement, along with a birdcage and the kitchen table. Even most of the family photos were left on the walls. Shifted to junk the moment we took off, left on the lawn in piles.

I left the mason jar caterpillar, who was still waiting to butterfly. Mindi never came to get Bear. O Touro never told her she was supposed to get him. For years Mindi would tell me that Bear was happy living on a farm and that his new family loved him. Sometimes I still wonder what Bear has been up to on that farm: dancing his dog dance, running around with a rock in his mouth.

Westview Place

O Touro maxed out at a buck twenty-five an hour and turned the radio knob until he got Rock 95 and blasted it nice and loud. The two of us hummed along and he butted a third or fourth or fifth cig into the hot and clipping Highway 11 winds. We took an exit and joined a procession of cottagers who arrived on the north side of Sunshine City, where a morass of corner gas stations and townhouse rows, apartments, and plazas greeted us. We continued along to West Street, where a convenience store, a doughnut shop, a Little Caesars, a store called Big Apple, and other unassuming businesses formed a semicircle plaza. The only place that had any consistent traffic besides the gas station was a slow-burning Timmies drive-thru and a stucco-themed KFC beside it. We came to a red.

"What's it like to live in an apartment?"

"You'll see," O Touro said. The light went green, and before I knew it we'd eased up and taken a right at a tiny sign with the ever straightforward WESTVIEW PLACE: NO VACANCY printed on it. O Touro raised a finger off the wheel. "We're up there. Sixth floor. Great view, bud. I'm telling you. You're gonna love it. You'll see."

He parked beside the lobby. "Wait in here until I'm back."

I grabbed the backpack, went out the passenger door, and waited. After five or ten minutes, a lady with the gait of Jack Sparrow and paint-stained clothes came from the closest apartment patio toward the truck, footballing a pack of du Mauriers under her arm. She had a ring of keys, and a heel occasionally slipped out of her sandals when she walked. Her name was Debbie, and I had met her briefly the night before when O Touro picked me up.

"Hi there, Cody! Excited to move in? Lot of kids here. Whole floors of them. Can't even count 'em on both hands. That's life as a super."

"What's a super?"

"Superintendent," Debbie said. "I look after the place. Keep it shipshape. Around here, everybody needs a hand now and then. Plus, I like to know my tenants quite well. But I also make collages and read, you know?"

"What's a tenant?"

"That's you and your father and your sister. C'mon. Let's go. Got you guys up in unit 606. When your pizza comes, they buzz 606 to get ahold of you. Then you let them up. Idiot-proof."

She let me in with her ring of keys and O Touro came around the hallway. They let me press the arrow pointing up, which kicked off a whirr that finished when one of the elevators opened for us. There was no ding like in the movies. We went in and held on to a metal bar that stuck out from the panelling. O Touro and Debbie let me press 6, and the elevator jutted up and up and up until it stopped and opened to a fire extinguisher hanging off the wall. The stink of a million cigs smoked on this floor alone rushed into the elevator and the smell was awfully cozy. Almost like I'd known it my whole life.

We walked along the hall and halted at unit 606. O Touro balanced the box he carried against the door, reached into his jeans pocket, yanked out a solo key, and unlocked the green door. Inside was a butt-naked main room and a nesting-doll L-shaped kitchen, with a little window and an open balcony door that let the breeze in. There were little cobwebs blowing in the corners and burn marks in the carpet. I followed O Touro around while he checked out the unit.

"Yours is on the right. Master bedroom."

It already had a few grocery boxes and two beds sitting in it, which made it feel small. The two of us took a couple trips, and then O Touro went to go get Kris while Debbie watched over me.

Us three had arranged the furniture by the evening's end. O Touro was sitting on the piss-whiff couch, sipping a Molson and taking a much-needed break.

"Where's your bedroom?" I asked.

"You're looking at it, bud." He smacked the cushion. "Have you checked out the view from this place?"

O Touro lifted himself off the couch real slow, which he did ever since the logs he sawed began falling on him. Before we stepped out onto the concrete, he looked me right in the eyes.

"Listen up. Whenever you're out here, I want you hanging on to this railing, all right? Don't lean over it. Don't toss anything off it. Don't get any funny ideas."

"Why would I?"

"Cuz you're my son, bud. Telling you."

I followed him out and held on to two bars, peering between them. In the immediate foreground was the Westview Place parking lot, and in the distance was the Sunshine City Square Mall and a Zellers and a Canadian Tire and a stream of cars whipping down Highway 11. A slightly nicer apartment across the street foregrounded our sunset. The Timmies car lineup remained steady.

"What you think? For real," he asked.

"It's beautiful."

"Sure is."

"Tomorrow I'm getting a cable guy in here. Then we're going to Food Basic$ to get some groceries. It's gonna be better this time. Telling you." The cig smoke blew away with the evening breeze.

That night I met the boy from one unit over, Vandy, who was a couple years older than me and had moles in funny places. We stayed up late playing *Super Smash Bros.* and rounds of Yu-Gi-Oh! while Debbie and O Touro and Vandy's mom chilled on the balcony, having a good laugh and a few beers. Kris decorated her room, which Debbie and O Touro promised her they would paint yellow and they did, albeit while drunk.

The adults stayed camped out on the balcony all night, and it wasn't too long before us kids passed out in front of The Plasma. Vandy snored.

Memory Card

O Touro shook me awake. “Good morning, bud.”

The heat stuffed both nostrils and had me choked in the throat for something to drink. I slowly peeled myself off the piss-whiff. Vandy was nowhere in sight.

“He went fishing with his grandpa,” O Touro said from the kitchen. “Think you’re ever gonna eat something or what?”

He came out of the kitchen with a steaming plate of bacon and eggs on the sunny side, with an orange slice wedged in the corner. I ate while O Touro lit a cig on the balcony. When I finished I dropped the plate in the sink and joined him. He lit another cig as cars pulled in and out of the parking lot down below.

“We need to go fishing sometime soon,” O Touro said.

“I don’t know anything about fishing.”

“Don’t worry, dude, I’ll teach you. Fishing is what the Portuguese know best. It’s in your blood. Telling you. Wanna go for a ride? Time I took you shopping.”

We stopped first at the Zellers. We walked to the electronics section at the back end and O Touro told the clerk he wanted to buy me a PlayStation 2. He let me pick out any game I wanted. Still high off finishing *Final Fantasy IX*, I bought a similar-looking RPG called *Star Ocean: Till the End of Time*, the subtitle of which was how happy I felt that day.

After, we drove along West Street listening to Rock 95 and ended up at a hock shop in downtown Sunshine City, basically a store-sized treasure chest. Guitars and jewellery and stereos and dusty tags and displays lined the inside. Everything was previously used. They also had used video games: Xbox games, Super Nintendo games, N64 games, PlayStation 2 games. O Touro pointed to the used PlayStation 2 games displayed in a tall glass case and told me to pick some out. After I did, my mind still blown, he got the store guy who he somehow already knew by name to carry them up to the register. Then we stopped by Food Basic$ in West Ridge and did a quick Beer Store run before heading home.

Back at Westview I made a beeline for The Plasma and began setting up the new PlayStation 2, plugging the coloured cables into their respective auxiliary inputs and flipping the TV channels until the AUX popped up in the top corner of the screen. I played for a few hours before I realized we forgot to buy a memory card. But O Touro was already drinking out on the balcony with the neighbours, so I just kept the PlayStation running.

I spent the next few days with Vandy and his little sister: helping deliver stacks of the *Packet & Times* on Vandy's route, hitting the beach, and playing grounders on the school jungle gym behind the apartment. They were my first guides through Sunshine City, taking me on a tour to the corner store and the plaza, where we bought our favourite chocolate bars and nacho cheese Doritos.

Their unit was low-lit and musty, with enough treasures to open at least a couple hock shops. Stacks of books and VHS tapes and newspaper clippings that went to the ceiling and back again. Two cats emerged from the clutter: a skinny one that skittered around the living room and a fat one eating kibble from a bowl. Next to their L-shaped kitchen was a makeshift room for his little sister, made possible by two bookshelves and a well-placed sheet. The lack of space in the walkways made the apartment seem all the littler.

I followed Vandy to his room, which was no different than the rest of the place except that his accumulation of kitsch was game-themed. He had a locker that he claimed was full of treasure and also a loonie collector he began filling long ago. Said he was saving for a new console.

We sat on the edge of his bed and played Nintendo for a couple hours. At one point he paused the game, brought me over to his dresser, and opened the middle drawer. It was packed with what look liked thousands of Halloween mini candies, chocolate bars, and Jolly Ranchers. We each grabbed a handful. Some of the hard candies were soft and the soft candies hard. I asked him if it was time to rip open the Doritos. I tore the bag and was hit with a wave of the most wizardly stink in the entire universe. Vandy ate the chips improperly, like me. The first few handfuls dusted up our fingers, and I licked the orange flavouring from under the nail. Then I pulled out a Dorito that had curled into itself like it was keeping secrets.

"No fucking way. That's a wish chip you got. Only come in some bags. Finder gets one wish, but that wish always comes true. Trust me, dude. One time I got a wish chip and it changed my life. I wished for a Nintendo and guess what? What we playing on? That's right. I've only seen one my whole life."

I stared at the chip, closed both eyes, and wished for an Xbox.

A couple days later, O Touro threw a mini birthday party for himself on our balcony. Vandy and his sister came over and we began playing a two-player game, which made her cry. After an hour of us being stuck on the same level, O Touro came inside and hugged me up off the couch crying. His face had turned a serious red, but he smiled between his cries, wailing louder than the surrounding sounds. He squeezed me tighter than he ever did before, and I could see that Vandy had gone back to playing the game and minding his business.

"Don't know how much I love you? You know that, right? I love you more than anything," O Touro said. "You mean so much to me. Don't you ever forget."

"I know you do, Dad. Why you crying?"

"Cuz I'm so happy to have you here, bud."

It was the first and maybe only time I ever saw O Touro cry. Afterwards he went back out onto the patio to drink another cold one. I started to wonder if his memory card was full.

The Bull

Before O Touro's O Touro, Velhote, met and married Avó Maria, he was just a Porto homegrown who'd dreamt of better citrus to squeeze and moved to São Miguel to find them. But to grow bitter and wither away on the faults of volcanic magma, a refuge of freguesias and villas built on strips of rock that sprawled and cooled along the lush rifts in the terra, was not Velhote's idea of the good life. Cuz Velhote didn't grab life by the horns. Velhote was the horns.

In the summer of 1962 in São Miguel, Avó Maria gave birth to O Touro in the toilet, and then his twin in the bedroom. Or so says O Touro.

Along came baby three one year later. One year after that, on Boxing Day, Avó Maria flew with her three children to Montreal, and later moved to a house in Kensington Market in Toronto. They had baby number four two years later.

O Touro said Velhote ran the Kensington Market house like a

farm. Of course, the family scaled and salted their own fish, churned goat's cheese, pack-wrapped sausages, gutted rabbits, split chickens in two—what are you, stupid? The basement had a cantina, kids could dance on grapes. There were two rules: dance on the grapes, inside before the streetlights turn on. When they're on, be in bed. New country. My rules.

O Touro first broke the rules shortly after he turned four. Got on the tricycle and took off down the lane, but when he came home, his bike got trashed and he got smacked across the face. Then O Touro told me how Avó Maria got her eyes. Said they got them at the same time.

See Avó Maria in the basement, trying to hide behind the furnace, begging O Touro to come hide, too. C'mon son, 'urry up.

Avó had O Touro stand in front of her. But all this meant was they could hear him together, slamming doors until he found their hiding spot. And Velhote didn't care if O Touro was in front of Avó. Velhote hit him for getting in the way. Again and again.

The Kensington Market house made O Touro levitate. Velhote threw him against walls, up the stairs, down them. Daily belts and high-rise boots turned into rugburn killjoy. There was a rifle pressed into his forehead when he was seven cuz the buckle is always coming. Telling you.

"My dad always told me it was my fault," O Touro says. "That I was the reason bad things happened to me.

"One afternoon I went to visit him when he was working on a high-rise in Parkdale. I was so excited to see him and to see what he did for a living, and he took one look at me and told me to go the fuck home. He beat me later that night.

"But I never let him stop me from living a normal life. Every day, I'd take off as far as I could from that house in Kensington and would end up in Bickford Park. I played hide-and-seek, on the jungle gym, basically with anybody who'd play with me. But I wasn't supposed to go too far. I remember once I cut my eye on a car window and ended up in the hospital and had to get stitches. He beat me later that night.

"But then his work picked up. He worked until he bought another home. Worked on the CN Tower. Worked himself up to a senior role, good pay. But one day he fell off a work site, landed on his leg, and got some insurance money. He and my mother separated shortly after. Think it was sometime in the fall. But their separation didn't keep him away. Courts told him to beat it, but he'd still find her. Didn't stop until the cops came. Didn't matter if he had a bad leg or not. Didn't matter if it was winter. It didn't matter because he was a man in the sixties and he did what he wanted.

"We ran as fast as the five of us could run and wherever we could all fit: cockroach apartments, single rooms, shelters. Dozens of moves, son. No window to make friends, even in a big city like Toronto. Friends were out of the question. I failed the second grade because of all that moving. For years, we ate cookies dipped in coffee and buttered bread for breakfast.

"When I was eleven I had to start working. I got a job making fifty cents a trip per courier, delivering papers, prescription drugs, you name it. When I was twelve, I found a second job making rails and earning two hundred and fifty bucks a week, giving my mom two hundred of it and keeping fifty bucks for myself. But I had to leave after the boss tried to date my sister.

"It was around then my mom got a job as a call girl and began bringing men into our house. Most of them were sickos. Came on to us. We were too young to do anything about it, son. And then she began dating one of them. His name was Tony: this name-calling, woman-beating, moving-into-the-home, I-eat-first motherfucker Tony.

"I beat the shit out of Tony the summer I turned thirteen. I don't know what I did but I remember seeing his front teeth on the kitchen floor. Blood all over the cabinets, the tablecloth. It made my head spin. I took everything I had in me out on him. My twin sister and brothers screamed at me. My mother's freaking out and tells me to get the fuck out. So I took off to the west end and ended up in this shelter in Parkdale, just around the corner from that high-rise he'd been working on. After the shelter, I moved in with a woman from Switzerland who charged me a hundred bucks a month for rent.

"I remember Velhote came to visit me. He came up to my room and took one look at the mattress and my bag of clothes and my size nine work boots and started mocking me. He goes, 'Why you sleeping on the floor? You a dog now?' I told him to go fuck himself. Want to be a dad now, huh? Now's your time? But of course, he didn't want to be a dad. He never wanted to be a dad.

"The one thing I've always had on my side was that I'm physically fit. Osler Public School let me pick between hockey and swimming. I liked hockey, but the gym teachers and trainers recognized I was good at swimming, which I'd been since I was a kid. They recruited me as captain of the team. I was so proud of myself for that. I held the city record at crossing a hundred-metre freestyle in fifty-two seconds, which was three seconds behind the world record at the time, believe it or not. They brought me to the Olympic team in Etobicoke and trained me daily. But my family never came to my swim meets. And then I remember asking my mom where my swim trophies were after one of those moves we did, and she told me we didn't need them so she left them behind at the last place. So I quit swimming and found dancing.

"I have a natural boogie in me. So natural I started teaching kids my age to dance in the school terrace. I learned how to waltz, dance on roller skates, bust a move during track and field. But I could also fight anytime other kids made me feel the way Tony or Velhote or those sickos in my mother's bed made me feel. I fought a lot, and moved to St. Luigi Catholic. And it wasn't long before St. Luigi Catholic gave me the boot and I had to move to Perth Avenue Public. Then after that I moved to Bloor Collegiate, an academic school that told me on the first day I'd never make it to college. I failed ninth grade twice. Never thought I'd make it to grade thirteen.

"But boy did I try. I forced myself to study as hard as I could and pass my finals every year. I knew my little brother was about to enter high school. And when he arrived at Bloor Collegiate, I became leader of a pack of bullies so they wouldn't fuck with him. Me and the vice-principal had frequent meetings whenever I showed up to school late. We would have coffee together. We were close. He'd ask me how I was doing at home and I'd tell him. But my brother began getting in trouble. I remember walking out of that office and then him walking in and the vice-principal getting himself worked up on seeing another one of us.

"I missed enough classes for Bloor Collegiate to give me the boot, and I dropped out of school at grade nine. After that, I worked at a doughnut shop at Dufferin and Bloor. Even got my little brother a job there too. Not to mention the owner got old and let me help more with the business. I think I stole something like nine grand out of the till over the course of two years. I wanted more money, so I had a couple guys doing small-time jewellery gigs for me, bringing me gold to sell at pawnshops. But one of those fuckers ratted me out, and I had to move to West Toronto Collegiate, which was brand-new then. I loved it. And then one day, when I was in my first-period class, the vice-principal pulled me into his office. But unlike the last vice-principal, this guy didn't like me very much. He tossed me my first warning. Told me the cops were looking for me. Already on their way to the school. Told me one of the guys got arrested and implicated me as his defence. Little fucker. The vice told me to call my mother. So I did.

"They never showed up. But me and my mom walked into the station together that day. I just lied. Fed them some bullshit. Told them I bought the gold off somebody else. They called me a lucky prick and told me to get out of there.

"I ended up in jail for a bit. Got out and developed a habit. I got good at breaking into houses and stores near my apartment on Bloor and Clinton. I began working for a guy and dating his niece. Those jobs the guy had me do were fun and simple. Sell gold. Sell jewellery and clothing to the poor or resell it to the refurbished shops in Chinatown. Steal trucks entirely or take everything I could off them. Tractor-trailer jobs.

"But all this shit meant I went crazy. I went lonely. I went lonely dating my boss's niece, and then I met Jackie. I loved Jackie enough to leave the niece. I remember the two of us going skating on rinks in Dufferin and making plans to get married. But she got pregnant in high school and had to abort the baby. Messed things up. Went crazy. A year later, I caught her fooling around with another guy. Ended up in jail for domestic assault when I was seventeen. The day I got out I overdosed on pills and came upon a white, bright light that took me someplace else.

"I woke up in a hospital bed with Jackie beside me in a fury. Screaming at me. Everybody's always screaming at me. She was asking me why the fuck I would do that to her. Do any of it to her. And I didn't know. Still don't. She wanted answers I couldn't provide. I was so in love with her but I didn't know what to say. So I just said sorry. I told her it wasn't who I wanted to be. Because it wasn't. That's the truth, son. None of this was who I wanted to be. I cried as hard as I ever cried and I told her over and over again it was the truth. But she didn't believe me and she left.

"After I got out of the hospital, I found a cheap-change basement apartment on Robinson Avenue. I got a job working at Ontario Place, the Exhibition, Royal York Hotel, a lighting store, and a Mac's Milk right next to it. Used to steal lottery tickets but lost on every single one. No cameras back then.

"Then I was twenty and got into a lot of trouble. Dealing and pimping and shit. I had long hair, tight jeans, and gold rings on each finger. Very John Travolta. That's when I met Donna. After a few weeks, I moved into her apartment in the Beaches. Renovated the whole thing for her.

"After living together for some time, she became my fiancée, the first of four fiancées. She gave me leather jackets with fox fur, which I wore every day. Even though she was a great woman, I got abusive with her at times. We broke up but continued to talk on weekends. And that's when my life went downhill.

"I got my grade twelve equivalency in pre-business and commerce and almost graduated with honours. I went to George Brown and took a fuckload of marketing and computer courses. I had a couple girls going crazy for me. One of them, this young Jewish girl, paid me to have sex with her. That's right, she paid me to have sex with her. I asked her for three hundred bucks and we went back to my place. She tossed me the cash after but wanted to go again, so I said no, I want more money. She shook her head because she didn't have any and when she shook it, I saw a diamond earring shining. It was thirty-five-carat diamond, high quality. Knew that'd be worth a bit, so I ended up doing it again for that earring. Turned out it was worth four thousand dollars. That earring stayed with me for a long time. I made your mother her engagement ring with that diamond.

"After George Brown, I moved to this place on Davenport and Dufferin. Me and my buddies went to every concert we could afford. Beach Boys, Pink Floyd, Supertramp, ZZ Top. We cried on coke when John Bonham died in 1980. All thanks to our best bud Giuseppe. We'd be sitting in a coffee shop with fifty cents in our pockets like broke-asses and Giuseppe would toss us tickets he got for twelve bucks. Plus we had a buddy who worked at Maple Leaf Gardens. Before shows, we'd smoke a bit of hash or whatever we could get our hands on.

"In 1980, we went to see the Rolling Stones for ninety bucks in Buffalo. The three of us took the bus from Toronto and grabbed a hotel room for dirt cheap, and when we got home later that night, we discovered our key fit every room on our floor. We trashed the entire hotel. We threw mattresses out windows and let off fire extinguishers. The next day was the concert, and us three were only fifteen rows back and eventually worked our way up front to the stage. We were right before the barriers, drinking moonshine and chasing it with vodka. My buddy caught a rose from Mick.

"Three years later, us and some friends headed to Florida for spring break. We stayed for one week and snorted as much cocaine as we could get our hands on, came back home wanting more.

"Then I was in bed when my phone rang rang rang. It was my brother, asking me to go back for a second trip. I said no since I was dead broke from the first trip. But Cathy, who I began seeing after Donna, tossed me sixty bucks. So I went again.

"We met biker chicks and got free drinks and lived it up, son. Telling you. On the first night, I punched the hotelier out and threw him in the pool. People were screaming at me, so I slipped out the back door to my room. I ended up meeting up with a few different women that week, all back to back.

"We stayed in Florida for a month and a half. Few different hotels. Eventually we were flat broke. My brother needed to fork out more money. I sold blow in Florida for a week for a man named Paolo. But of course that didn't work out. So we had to head back. And that's when my life went downhill.

"Back home, I kept afloat selling blow to live in this cockroach apartment in Lansdowne in the eighties. I even taught my girlfriends how to dance as strippers. When people owed me money, I broke into their place and waited for them to come home. I broke into stores and paid rent through more tractor-trailer jobs. I ended up in jail five times.

"I knew I didn't want to do it anymore.

"Before your uncle Rob was a farmer, he was a gang member from the east side of the city, Regent Parkish. He'd made a name for himself. Even though we were in opposite gangs, our paths crossed often and we heard a lot about each other. Eventually, we learned we shared a lot of similarities and became best friends. We got a place together at St. Clair and Old Weston Road. We dressed up nice, went clubbing and bar-hopping almost every night. Our favourite joint was this place on Bloor called Connections. It was a disco bar above a strip club called Hollywoods. A good one, too. And when I was twenty-two, I got job at Hollywoods as a stripper and began making some cash as a dancer, an escort, a coke dealer, a pimp, and a gang member, among a few other things. One night, Rob and I were at Connections when this group of chicks walked in. I immediately went for the first one I saw. I asked her what her name was and she told me it was Janice. You remember Janice, right? Janice who lived on the highway with Pete? They had that pet pig? Anyways, Janice wasn't buying my offer and got up to get a drink from the bar. So I went up to the girl beside her. She had tanned skin, long dark curls, and her makeup was all done up. Guess who that was? Your mother and I began dating right away. She moved in with me and Uncle Rob. We got married a year later. I wore a white tux. Isn't that something?"

Count Your Wish Chips

A couple days after O Touro's memory card overloaded, he called me out to the balcony and handed me the phone. It was Julian. The heartbeat looked sleepy, and I watched it for the entire call.

"Dude," I said. "Got so much to tell you. Won't believe it. How's Alliston?"

"Oh you know. School sucks. Just a bunch of rich kids here. I made one friend, but he's a Korean exchange student and has to move back home soon. Least I have a job and a room, though. You packed up the games, right?"

"Yes. Plus Dad bought a PlayStation 2 and a bunch of new ones. Even made some friends. I think you'll like it here. When you coming?"

"I don't know, Cody."

"Well, I hope you know soon."

"Me too. I gotta go eat dinner now. They're calling me."

"All right. Love you, man."

"Love you, too."

It was the first time we'd ever said it.

Vandy introduced me to all the half-bads at Westview. The group of us became friends and played grounders in the schoolyard out back and took day trips to Wasaga Beach with O Touro and Vandy's mom. We held epic wrestling matches in the school field and ran up and down the staircases and rode our bikes around the neighbourhood.

At the Orchard Park playground, we met Deanie Boy. Deanie Boy lived on the third floor, on the opposite side of the hallway, so his balcony faced the car lot out back and Orchard Park just beyond it. His family hung dreamcatchers in the windows and pan-NDN blankets with eagles and neechies in wolf hats, the ones you buy at corner stores and flea markets, and they brought me to pow-wows and family gatherings in Rama. He had an Xbox and the Duke controllers—the classic original-release model—before the rest of us. I always liked it at Deanie Boy's place cuz his mom fed me spicy Jamaican beef patties and homemade hangover soup and endless bowls of cereal.

Most days that fall we spent together in and around Westview. Over time, we developed a drop in, drop out situation among our collective apartments. Each of our homes became the other's home, and it eventually began to feel like one house broken up across different floors. We'd invite one another over for holiday dinners that gave me canker sores. One day, Vandy's mom procured him a set of wooden guns that shot elastics and almost immediately we began shooting them off.

I was in the middle of one of those elastic gun fights a little before Christmas, when I had to run home to grab a snack. I opened the door and holy cow who was it but Julian, standing next to the couch. Still had his coat on. We hugged and he told me he was moving in and pointed to a bag. Said it was his present for me this year. I unzipped it and saw the one and only green-and-black machine, along with *Halo 2* and a set of controllers. Saved every paycheque to buy that Xbox.

"I beat the campaign," he told me. "Ending's a bullshit cliff-hanger. You'll see. Must have left it like that so they could make a sequel. Bastards."

"I'm not gonna be mad if there's another *Halo* in the world, though."

We spent the winter playing that game. All I'm going to say is count your wish chips.

My Brother's Place

I never picked up the phone when it rang. The missed calls log usually showed the usual suspects: Deanie Boy, Rogers, Bell, Patrick Fogarty Catholic Secondary calling to report yet another absence. But I started to see calls from a contact named My Brother's Place.

At first I figured it was one of O Touro's brothers. The number popped up again and again, and whenever O Touro picked up he spoke from the top of his throat. He'd talk for hours laughing his ass off and mentioning parts of his past he'd never told me about.

One day, O Touro called me into the living room. He was chilling on the couch, and the phone was tucked between his hands. A pack of du Mauriers next to the wallet like always. Receipts poking out the top of the wallet. CNN ticker on The Plasma.

"Son, what you want for Christmas this year?"

"Snowboard." The *Packet & Times* came with flyers advertising rows of sleek boards with vibrant designs splashed on their undersides. I knew most of them would cost O Touro a good chunk of his Hydro One paycheque, but Julian had one and I had to push for it so that we could race down a mountain together.

"Well if a snowboard is what you want, a snowboard is what you're getting. Telling you right now." He picked the phone back up and kept talking to My Brother's Place.

That night at dinner O Touro told me and Julian that we were spending Christmas at My Brother's Place. When Julian asked him what that was, he told us he knew My Brother's Place from when he was a little. And we knew better than to ask questions about when O Touro was little. Cuz to me he never was. Just went from born to O Touro.

When the day rolled around, we took Debbie's soft-top to Toronto and parked in a densely packed off-grid street. We hopped out of the convertible and followed O Touro up the porch. Before we opened the door and stepped into the lobby, I could already hear a hundred voices. O Touro pointed at a coat rack and said to make it fast cuz we got lots of people to meet.

A man burst through the crowd to bear-hug O Touro.

"How you been, [Brother]?"

"[Brother], bro, so good to see you! Is [Brother] here?"

"Just in the kitchen, [Brother]. I'll let him know you're here."

"[Brother], these are my sons."

We shook the brother's hand.

"Been hearing a lot about you two. You boys ready for Christmas or what?"

We nodded.

Julian and I walked down the hallway side by side. The place was packed with brothers. Young brothers playing Game Boys in the main room and old brothers with charming accents joking with one another in the kitchen and teenage brothers running around the place like the hyenas in *The Lion King*. Every brother looked close to every other brother, a tight-knit brotherhood.

Us two walked into the kitchen and sat down on two plastic chairs. Hours passed and we'd barely spoken to any of the other brothers. O Touro kept running around the main floor circulating and smiling and shaking every brother's hand like crazy. I kept wondering how he knew all these people. It seemed these brothers knew him better than he knew us and vice versa. I walked over to a pair of brothers with buzzed heads. They looked severe and tough and in charge, but still a bit littler than O Touro. I asked them where the washroom was.

"I think [Brother] is using the kitchen one. But you can use the one upstairs, [Brother]."

I pushed through groups of brothers in the hallway and went up a staircase until I hit the second floor. While I was waiting for a brother to finish in the bathroom, I noticed a room with an open door, so I stepped inside. Presents from the brothers, for the brothers, lined the walls. Every present had been wrapped with the same green wrapping paper. The name tags were written in the same handwriting. Only one was unwrapped. It was a red snowboard with plastic bindings built into the board that I recognized from our trips to Walmart. "Cody" on the tag. I heard the flush and running tap of the bathroom and hid behind the door until the creaking steps faded in the distance.

Shortly after, we had Christmas. Every brother piled into the living room. I couldn't see O Touro anywhere but could see Santa, who looked just like O Touro. He called me over and handed me the snowboard.

It would be years before I understood that the men at My Brother's Place were bound by their experience with the mental health system and not by blood. But O Touro did take us back to that area, shortly after Christmas, to visit his real brothers and sisters. Again we showed up to the city freezing in Debbie's soft-top, this time in the midst of a blizzard. O Touro spent the afternoon driving us around and throwing snowballs at the windows of houses that he last remembered his brothers and sisters living in. He yelled out their names and ran around the sides and front, knocking on the door and calling out to them, "C'mon, it's O Touro, c'mon, open up," before scooting back in the car, swearing under his breath.

On the way home, O Touro turned the heat off and our breath gathered in front of our faces. I fell asleep, and while I was passed out we hit empty. When I woke up, we were at a gas station somewhere off the highway. O Touro had to use a corner store phone to call Debbie to borrow her credit card number. We didn't get back to Westview Place until three or four in the morning, but O Touro carried me into the house like a newborn.

The Galaxy Deposit

Our first year at Westview went by quick. O Touro worked a shit ton, and on days off if he was in a good mood he'd zone out into the frying pan or wok and cook tasty stir-fry chicken-and-rice dishes that got heaped steaming onto my plate, or questionable cherry meatloaf that we ate in the dark for some reason, or soggy pasta dishes that he would catch me sneaking to the bathroom in my napkin. He let Kris smoke weed and would even roll her and her pals joints made from stashes he found working for Hydro One, and he let Julian have his tenth-grade buddies over whenever they needed a place to party.

In the spring, Kris began taking me to the library to sign out books and movies I'd forget to return. That year for my birthday, O Touro bought me the Lemony Snicket series from the Scholastic catalogue and showed up to my class with the book bag slung across his back. The littlest grin.

In the summer, O Touro took the Westview Placers to Grease Beach and to Wasaga Beach and to Roscoe's for ice cream. When he was out partying or working, the Placers and I would fill balloons with tap water until they got so huge and unstable we could barely throw them off the balcony to thwack six floors down by the trash room and Debbie's porch, us giggling by the time she poked her head out. When a group of Placers would come over for a sleepover, someone always waited until O Touro began snoring to put channel 32 on The Plasma, where the softcore porno of *Latin Lover* played muted and made us all quiet, too.

In the fall, the momentum sputtered but kept strong. O Touro made me sit in the living room for an afternoon to study for a spelling test worth five percent, cuz school is everything, bud. He painted the apartment a neutral beige and rearranged the furniture. We got internet installed and Julian showed me how to use MySpace, MSN, and LimeWire. O Touro took me and the Westview Placers to his buddies' apartments to watch the Leafs and play Risk all night.

By the time February rolled around there was frost on the bedroom windows that I liked to scrape off slowly with my fingernails. My eleventh birthday was only a few months away and I'd yet to tell Kris and Julian and O Touro about my plans for it. O Touro was busy with work and hadn't been home for a few days.

I thought about my eleventh birthday party almost every day for weeks. If the blueprint mapped out right, at least nine friends from my fifth-grade class could sleep over, but only if they slept side by side sardine on my bedroom floor. It could happen. Space was limited but we always made it work. Plus I had a bulletproof plan: the

Westview Placers would stay for the party and go back to their apartments after so that the classmates could crash in unit 606. Everybody could play hide-and-seek across the apartment property. We'd have cake and endless bowls of ice cream, and at night we'd go get chocolate bars and Doritos from the plaza corner store. Everybody would get a turn playing *Halo 2* on The Plasma, and we'd pin up blankets to prevent screen peeking, which is when a player peeks at their opponent's screen to get an advantage. Julian would help me curate a playlist with songs downloaded off LimeWire. Kris would take us on drives around town in a Lexus or Lambo. I'd even find a way to hide the beer stain on the *Halo 2* cover, which appeared after O Touro had a night of the good life. I was set to have the best birthday I'd ever had. I just hadn't mentioned it to anyone yet.

I sat next to Kris at the living room table, where she was finishing a bowl of Honeycombs, and told her about the blueprint. She nodded and chewed and swallowed, waited for me to finish.

"I like it! But I don't know, Code," she said. She finished the bowl and took it to the sink. "Dad might say no to that many of you guys running around the place."

Dismayed, I continued a rip in our vinyl tablecloth. None of us three had had a real birthday party with friends in a while. For Julian's birthday that year, Kris spent the day trying to cheer him up and together us three walked to the store to get pop and chips for a movie. O Touro phoned in the afternoon to tell us he was bringing home pizza but he never showed up, and us three went to bed without dinner. O Touro wouldn't show up for three, four days at a time, only giving Kris enough money for my lunches so that I could show up to class with food.

"Never mind, then. It's all good."

It was then that her brows raised, like O Touro's do when he gets an idea in his head. "You want a good party? Fine. I'll help you throw the best birthday party you've ever had."

"Where, then?"

She hmmed. "What about Galaxy, in West Ridge? They do birthdays, and they have that game room. Pretty sure they could rent you a cinema, too."

"Do it, dude," Julian said from the computer, ripping a leaked MP3. "Invite all the girls from your grade and tell them presents are mandatory."

Right around then O Touro came home and carried the winter in with him. In his Hydro One safety vest, easy-fit work pants, super-sized mesh gloves, and wet steel-toes, he opened and closed the front door and dropped his lunchbox beside The Plasma. He began to take parts of his outfit off in different places around the apartment. A solid five o'clock shadow mossed along his face. His eyes, the same deep brown he gave us three, were full of the sleeps. His laboured gait made him gasp in pain, like always when he sat down too fast on the couch.

"Why aren't you guys in school?"

"Snow day," Julian said.

O Touro coughed a fit and sighed out of it. "Wish I had a snow day for work. Would be nice."

"I want to have a birthday party this year," I said.

"Oh yeah? Ha. And where's that taking place?"

"The Galaxy Cinemas."

"Come on, Dad," Kris said. "Cody wants it. We'll help him plan."

"You know what? You're lucky it's not for a bit cuz if you really want it, you're going to get it. Telling you." He nodded, walked to the bathroom, and turned on the shower.

"Don't worry," Kris whispered. "I'll keep on him."

We planned everything. Every detail. Kris convinced O Touro to agree to putting a deposit down for the Galaxy party space and rent out a cinema. She went to the dollar store for balloons and got a friend to drive her to Walmart to pick up the invitations. She broke down how many friends I could invite and helped me pick the cutest girls in the class picture. That one. She's cute. What's her name? Pick her. No. Not her.

She wrote out the names on each envelope in elegant cursive and included the event description inside. She and Julian picked out a list of movies playing on the Saturday, my actual birthday. We decided on *Scary Movie 4*.

On April Fool's Day, a mix of truck salt and heat from the heartbeat broke the blanket of snow into slush that soaked through my Airwalks to the toes. It was so hot that our winter coats were in the closet and on the backs of our doors later that day.

I walked to Monsignor Lee Catholic Elementary with thirty lime-green envelopes, shuffling them over and over. I handed them out at lunchtime until nearly every kid in class had a green rectangle on their desk. After I was done, I sat down and pulled out that day's lunch, which like always was some last-minute sandwich, a slice of bologna tucked in between two corner pieces of Wonder Bread or a slice of Little Caesars carefully wrapped in paper towel. O Touro started out the school year strong, buying enough groceries to fill the kitchen, but this effort had puttered out.

"Cody, how the hell you going to afford a party at the Galaxy if you can't even bring a proper lunch?" asked a class bro, prompting a corner of kids to giggle. I giggled with them cuz that's what half-bads do. And maybe the bro had a point. The day March Break started, I'd gotten in an MSN Messenger fight with a deskmate who threatened to call Children's Aid on me. He said the whole class knew what was going on, and then he blocked me.

A few weeks before the party, I woke up to Kris and O Touro having a yellfight in the living room.

"You know what? Why don't you pay the bills in this place and tell me how easy it is to raise three kids on your own with no help from your [see-you-next-Tuesday] of a mother. Who by the way is supposed to be paying me fucking support right now. About time I take her to court."

"Guess you forgot who took care of things while you were gone. And yeah. Maybe one day I will pay the bills and guess what? I'll pay them on time. Wouldn't that be something? Point is, you made a promise to your kid. He needs this. You do this and you fuck up. Again and again."

When I stepped into the living room red-face shameful, I could see the balcony sliding glass was open and O Touro was letting the cig stink out and the cold air in. There was a Molson on the table, and he picked it up and sipped a big sip. The last houseplant from Happyland—the one O Touro and Mindi got before I was born—remained faithful in the corner and listened to us three intently. I asked them if they were fighting about the party or what, and they both stopped and looked at me. O Touro said look, bud, got no money to pay that deposit but I promise I will after this next pay.

"But they need the deposit soon, don't they?"

"Well I'll fucking tell them to wait, dude. Promise you that much. Telling you."

A week or two before the party, O Touro's face pressed into Julian's after Julian began calling O Touro by his birth name. O Touro backed him up against the wall and told him he was gonna knock him out. Kris bolted out of bed to see what was going on. O Touro told her he knew Mindi was talking to us three on MSN Messenger, which he found out after he made me log in to my account. Kris told him the truth would come out that he was using again, that he'd show up completely zonked and unable to stand up, that us three would wake up with crackheads passed out on the couch, that he was working all week and then spending Thursday to Sunday partying with the chicks he blew his money on, only to stop back at the apartment to hand us a measly ninety bucks for food. She reminded him that's why I didn't get the party and that's why we had an empty fridge.

It wasn't until the morning of my birthday that I found out the Galaxy never received a deposit of any kind. I got anxious and spent the day beating the *Halo 2* campaign. Again. Not to mention that O Touro hadn't come home for a few days and counting. When Kris got home that evening, she was all kinds of pissed off.

"It's okay, don't worry, just chill," Julian said. "I didn't have a birthday party this year anyways. And who cares? It's just a birthday. Birthdays are just other days. Let's go play a game."

"No, it's not okay," Kris said. "It's not about the fucking movie theatre. Look at this place. We can't even take him out to dinner, Julian."

Kris went to the kitchen and came out with three bowls of Kraft Dinner in ten minutes. She mixed the cheese powder with water cuz there was no milk. Ran out of ketchup on the first bowl. We sat around the coffee table and ate in silence. It wasn't until I got into bed that I realized I hadn't told anybody the party was cancelled. But it was okay, cuz on Monday I found out that most of the kids I invited never planned on actually showing up to the Galaxy anyway.

A few weeks later, I was called into the principal's office, where I had the first of many conversations with a Children's Aid worker named Theresa. Seemed that MSN fight had cast a spell on me. Theresa calmly introduced herself and asked me a bunch of questions about what the future might look like at Westview Place. I told her everything was all right, that this was the good life. As far as I was concerned, living in an apartment building was dope. We had a buzzer on a wall and could throw garbage down a chute in the hallway. Sure, O Touro had done a big do or two, but even with his bad back he slept on a couch so that us three could have beds. I said that if anything, Kris was old enough to take care of me and Julian, and that I planned to move in with her anyways. Theresa agreed it was a good idea. She was as sweet as any agent of the state could be.

Rage Quit

Another player's body got shot on the TV screen. Deanie Boy was pumped and buttering himself up, and sure enough the multiplayer announcer in *Halo 2* confirmed that he was indeed on a killing spree, which you get if you kill five people without dying. Five Codys. I was cheesed. Deanie Boy played a good game of *Halo 2*, better than me or anybody else in the building. He could pick any Westview Placer clean off the map.

I spawned behind a staircase or some hunk of metal and immediately looked down at my feet. Deanie Boy was directly across from me, still in the lookout. Between us was a massive windmill turning slowly and in the distance was a beach, along with the rocket launcher, plasma grenades, and a Warthog. Deanie Boy's sniper bullets whizzed right by me, and I moved out of the way. He fired off twice again, the bullets swishing past me. I could see them piercing the windmill with holes that faded away after a few seconds and regenerated into fresh concrete. I followed the plank and hopped into the cog of the windmill to hide and grab an invisibility shield, which was the one chance to get Deanie Boy out of his lookout. From the metal plank I jumped two storeys and hit the dirt running. Us Westview Placers had to look at the ground to prevent screen peeking.

I was ready to end Deanie Boy's killing spree, but not ready enough, cuz the invisibility shield had been running low and slowly began to show an outline. Bullet connected to head. The announcer boomed over the TV speakers that it was game over.

"Yeah, buddy!"

"What the hell, man! You screen-peeked again."

"No I didn't, bro. You just suck at *Halo*," he said, jiggling and giggling at his version of the truth.

We played another round but Deanie Boy rage-quit, abruptly ending our match once I began to win. Julian showed up and wanted to play his snowboarding game, so Deanie Boy fist-bumped me and peaced out. After a couple runs down the mountain, Julian went to Kris's room to watch TV.

You know you're in phony company when they claim that everything goes quiet after the buckle comes. Cuz when the buckle comes, there's no mute button. When the buckle comes, it's the loudest thing in the world.

The night the cops came to unit 606 kicked off with a shoe. O Touro had recently told Kris that she better start working and paying rent now that she was eighteen, even though she was still in school and taking care of us. Told her he was done with her shit and that she couldn't have any friends or boyfriends over ever again. She told him he couldn't tell her what to do and that she was sick of the drugs and watching him spiral.

He called Kris a see-you-next-Tuesday, so she threw a shoe at him. O Touro told her he knew how to punch a woman without leaving a mark. He'd told that to Mindimooye, too.

He punched her. He was right.

Kris started having a panic attack, crying and calling him crazy. So O Touro called the cops. And when they showed up, they didn't believe her side of the story.

"My daughter's on a lot of meds, Officer. Effexor. All kinds. She's gonna kill herself. She assaulted me. She's bipolar."

The officers took Kris to a hospital and locked her in a room for the night. One of those padded rooms without a doorknob.

At some point, Mindi showed up to grab me and Julian, and us three drove in Chiclets' Jeep to her new apartment on Cedar Island Road. She told us we could take the next day off school.

We began sleeping at Mindi's, on the couches and the cushions of the couches on the floor. When Kris left the hospital she came and stayed there too, but that ended after a week, when Mindi and Chiclets came home shlammered at six in the morning with one of Chiclets' buddies, and Chiclets began ripping Mindi apart, calling her an idiot, saying that since the two of them split the boob job he owned one tit. The insults woke Kris up and she snapped on Chiclets.

Of course, this being a half-bad story, Mindi kicked Kris out after that, and she had to go live at a friend's place and go on student welfare to pay rent. And since the welfare made her attend class every day, her grades shot her up to the honour roll. But it wasn't long before she made up with O Touro, enough to go back to living in her old yellow bedroom at Westview Place.

Catfight

In Chiclets' Jeep, Mindi pulled up to the drive-thru ATM machine at the Trust in downtown Sunshine City. There was a credit card waiting in the slot for us when it was our turn. Mindi grabbed it, assessed it, and tossed it next to a pile of receipts, files, and legal papers on the dash. She slid her debit card into the machine.

"C'mon, c'mon," Mindi said. She poked her PIN into the screen. Accounts. Withdrawals. Mindi wanted a receipt. She poked the bank for her rent bill for Cedar Island Road, then smacked the wheel and fuck fuck fuck. No five hundred bucks for us. There was supposed to be some money, something, but nothing came out of the machine. Some type of freeze on her account. Whatever that means.

Us three had tried living—albeit unsuccessfully—in Mindi's one-bedroom on Cedar Island Road. But ever since Kris left, and Julian went to stay on his buddy Dyson's basement futon, we weren't clearing many withdrawals.

Mindi banked Chiclets' Jeep around the turn. She stopped beside a black SUV on the street.

The driver said, "I didn't leave my card in the ATM, did I?"

"Oh, yes. You certainly did. Would have took it, ha," Mindi said.

The driver didn't laugh back, rather looked at Mindi like she was a baddie, plucked the card from her reach, and drove off. We pulled over and parked on the curb, and I followed her into the Trust. She walked up to the tellers, who'd already begun closing.

"Sorry, ma'am. Bank's closed."

"Actually, you still have ten minutes, thanks," Mindi said. "So I'd like to know what's going on with my account. Now."

"I'm sorry?"

"You don't get it. I need that money. I need that money. Here's my card. Look up the account. Now. You still got ten minutes."

The teller stared at the other workers. She loaded up Mindi's account. "All right. Enter your PIN, please. Thank you. So it says you have a hold of some kind."

"'Some kind'? What do you mean 'some kind' of hold? It's money. Why's there a hold on my money?"

"I'm not sure. Maybe a cheque bounced?"

"You listen up, mmkay? I have nowhere for me and my son to live if I can't get that money. We don't have any way to eat. So I need you to fix it, since this is a fuckup on your end. That cheque went through. I know it did. I know I got paid. It's a big fucking company, understand?"

The teller just looked at the screen and back at Mindi and then the other tellers. "Sorry. I can't help you."

So Mindi stormed out, and I just stood there for a moment making eye contact with the tellers before running after her. She slammed the door and we sat in the Jeep for a minute.

"All right. We're gonna go to Lisa's for a bit."

Mindi said little all on the way to Bass Line, where Auntie Lisa lived. Auntie Lisa worked as a chef and was the ex of one of Mindi's casino serving buddies. When we arrived, we walked around the back like always and met Lisa at the patio door.

"How ya been, babe?" Lisa asked. "Not good, I'm guessing?"

"You know. It is what it is."

"You're telling me."

"Sounds like we need a couple drinks, eh?" Mindi said before she threw her head back laughing and her coat on the closest dining room chair. Rock 95 played from Lisa's surround sound that usually blasted VeggieTales for her kid. We sat between toy trucks and castles. Tonight it was just Lisa and Mindi and me and Lisa's buddy sitting in a semicircle on the floor, playing a drinking game called caps. To play caps, we each needed a bottle, so one of them finished a beer and let me fill the empty with water. We took turns chucking a spare cap at the caps crowning our bottles. Mindi tossed a cap at mine. She missed. They drank more and more and got halfway through the two-four and beat me at caps a lot. I got bored and moved to the couch and then Mindi came up to me.

"Go to bed."

"It's only nine though, Mom."

"It doesn't matter. You have school, babe. You know how important school is, don't you?"

"I want to use the phone."

"Oh you do, do you? Here then." Mindi got up and walked over to the phone and held it out to me. "Here's the phone. Just do it, fine, just call her. Call your sister. Just watch how fast this party shuts down. Just watch."

Before I pressed Call, Mindi took me by the shoulder and marched me upstairs to Lisa's bedroom. She turned the lights off, told me not to come out until the morning, and slammed the door goodnight. But I didn't know how Mindi expected me to fall asleep when they kept woo-girling in the living room and blasting Rock 95 as loud as they could. I sat in the dark and dialed Kris.

"Cody? Is that you? What's wrong?"

"You need to come get me," I said. "She's drunk, and we're at Lisa's and Mom's card got declined and then we played caps and now I'm in Lisa's room and the lights are off and I'm locked in."

She told me to stay there and not move.

When Kris finally arrived from Westview Place, I could only hear bits of things shouted over "Highway to Hell" booming on the radio.

"Where's Cody?"

"Get out, 'cha bitch. Nobody told you to come here," Mindi said.

"Actually, your son doesn't feel safe and called me."

I unlocked the door and caught a glimpse of them. Kris walked toward the stairs up to the bedroom. But Mindi kept trying to lift her leg, so Kris kicked her. And then Mindi pulled her down the stairs. And then Lisa and Lisa's bud began cheering, laughing at Mindi, yelling "Catfight!" and "Bitchfight!" Mindi and Kris were slamming each other into the ground like WWE. Mindi even pulled some of Kris's hair from her scalp. It looked like Mindi was winning.

I ran into Lisa's kid's old room and flipped on the lights. It had ocean-blue walls and was empty except for a tiny glowing fish tank in the corner. My hands shook as I picked up a bottle of fish flakes. My dumb ass thought fish flakes was the best way to kill myself at the time. I was over hearing Kris and Mindi call each other see-you-next-Tuesdays and smashing their heads together cuz of me. Just then Auntie Lisa stumbled in to check up.

"Cody . . . Oh geez. Calm down, buddy. It's okay!"

I told her nope it's not and that I wanted to do it. It was time for me to leave. I was eleven years old and ready to die cuz that's what's right when Kris and Mindi are rolling on the floor like esibanag fighting over trash on YouTube.

"Oh Cody. You can't kill yourself with fish food. All you'll do is turn into a fish! Blub blub blub."

She took me downstairs holding my hand. The lights had dimmed, but Kris and Mindi were still screaming at each other.

"Look at him," Kris said. "Look at him. Got your son having panic attacks already, eh? I'm gonna call the cops on you."

"You're going to call the cops? On me? NO. I'll call the cops on you!"

"You locked your son in a room."

"Too bad. I'm his mom. And you're not taking him. You do that and watch how fast this is over," Mindi said, ready to dial.

"Get out," Lisa said. "Or like your mother said, we're calling the cops."

Eventually Kris had no choice but to leave this standoff and go home. She pulled me in close and told me she loved me and that it would be okay. And of course it was. And then she left, and we turned on *Ice Age*, and I passed out in one of Lisa's kid's fluffy chairs.

One Brief Summer with Adam and Eve

After the big do at Lisa's, Kris swooped in to the rescue again. Kris had dropped out of high school for good and gotten a job at Casino Rama, was saving up her paycheques to finally get an apartment of her own. But the plan hit a snag when she mentioned to her shift supervisor that O Touro began using again, the very shift supervisor who had Mindi fired. The supervisor suggested she go to Children's Aid and offered Kris a ride. Following the visit, someone from the Children's Aid office called her and told her she had twenty-four hours to find a home for us or else they'd snatch me. After a day of frantic phone-calling, she found us a place with Adam and Eve, our godparents and old friends of Mindi and O Touro from back in their casino days who had a spare basement bedroom at their house in the Rama countryside.

We spent the evening packing up whatever we had left at Westview. After the night the buckle came, O Touro had removed any trace of us kids from the main room. It felt like a motel. There was a bowl of fruit that looked like a set piece—I imagined it superglued to the counter. O Touro drew back the curtains and opened the windows to let the June cool in, and fluffs and dust bunnies floated around in the pale light, and maybe it was something simple, like the updated tablecloth on the kitchen table, that made me realize I'd never have another O Touro stir-fry there again. And as with the other townhouse apartments and one-bedrooms and newly renovated dens and shaggy temporaries O Touro made cozy for us, the cleanliness of unit 606 on that day made it feel like there was nothing else to do but sit and be bored or lonely.

O Touro was resting his back on the couch but got up to hug me and ask how things were. I told him it would be a lot better if I knew what was happening.

"Me too, bud. Think I'm moving into Debbie's spare."

As we packed I lamented with Kris about how for a while at Westview it felt like we had it all figured out. She offered to buy me some Häagen-Dazs, her treat, and off we went one last time through the foyer doors and past the stacks and bags of newspapers, hitting a most beautiful sunset at the intersection. I found a ten-dollar bill on the sidewalk and Kris thought that was very lucky of me. We got on the juicy yet forsaken topic of back-to-school clothes and Kris reminded me that brand names were not important, even though we both knew they kinda were. At the lights, we watched cars whip down West Street to the highway. When we got back we finished packing and ate the entire tub of ice cream.

In the morning O Touro drove us out past Rama, up a sloped hill and then down it before pulling up to Adam and Eve's house. Eve waited in the driveway for us. We shuffled awkwardly on the pavement and hugged one another, then unloaded our stuff into the corner room at the end of their basement. There were two single beds, fresh linens, and a dresser in the corner. We picked our beds without enthusiasm of any kind. The carpet was olive and hard when you sat on it. And then we pretty much just said goodbye to O Touro in the driveway. Another hug. I waved him off, watching his truck pull out.

For dinner, Eve made veal parmesan, and then I played PlayStation with their son until it got dark enough for bedtime. But of course, I couldn't fall asleep. I just laid in bed and watched the morning light come through a tiny window on Kris's side of the room. A toilet flushed upstairs and the air-con turned on again, and when it stopped we coughed.

It didn't take me long to get used to the rhythms of life at Adam and Eve's. Adam took me through the garden and pointed out the perennials, taught me how to mow a lawn and whack a weed, how to disperse water evenly among the lilies and roses and rhododendrons and peonies. We camped in the backyard and they took me to see sizzling fireworks that lit up a packed waterfront on Canada Day. I learned how to ride a bike by going back and forth along the road to the nearby beach. When I connected with a tree stump and flipped over the handlebars, they bandaged up my elbows and knees. We went to Niagara Falls for a weekend getaway and to giant family reunions, and they even let me stand in the photos with them. On Sundays I went with their son to the homeschooled house across the street for bible study, where we practised the rosary in a candlelit living room with the curtains closed. One night Eve said "Come here" and brought me to her son's room, where he laid in bed, praying for me and Kris under his night lamp.

In July, O Touro came for a visit. He took me to Pet Valu, and I ran up and down the aisles looking for a lizard. Not a Komodo like the ones Julian said roamed the Eastside of Happyland on summer nights, but a little guy I could look after, maybe pimp out with some amber sand and bendy vines. O Touro wanted to get me a present to make up for hocking the PlayStation 2 a few months back.

"Which one you want, bud? What about this guy?"

He pointed to a real skinny one. Slits for vision and little Miss Frizzle lips. Cashier said it was the last crested they had in stock and asked if I wanted to hold him, and I told her yes, I would, thank you very much.

He was easy to hold. Didn't need a heat lamp or a fish bowl. As usual, O Touro put his first-class haggle to use. O Touro had the eyes for the deal, was always slinging some next-level bullshit to get out of paying for a breakfast I was already three-quarters into ("Why aren't you eating it, bud? You're looking sick. Eggs gone bad or cold or what is it?"), lest we leave with him yelling his loyalty lost out the door, me trailing after.

Back at the truck I watched him secure the vertical cage, bendy vines, fake ivy, and a singing cricket crate into the back seat beside the boxed gecko. I came up with Iggy's name on the drive back to Adam and Eve's. "Hope you like your lizard, son. Best I can do for now. Telling you."

I didn't see O Touro again until August, when he came for a beach day. Us two pork chops swam out far past the shallow end and played Frisbee with two Sunshine City teenagers cuz O Touro had the ability to chat up just about anybody. We tossed it back and forth and cracked jokes, and O Touro listened to me yap about video games and Adam and Eve and their garden.

When I got back to Adam and Eve's, there was a van in the driveway and out stepped Julian. I hadn't seen him in months, since he started sleeping at his buddy Dyson's. He was taller and had grown his hair out a bit and was even wearing new clothes.

"Shit . . . Cody, is that you?" Julian grabbed my arm and examined it. I hadn't noticed, but the heartbeat had soaked me for hours and hours. "How'd you get so dark?"

"Dad took me to the beach."

Sure enough, the tan was gone the first week of fall, when a Jeep I'd seen before pulled into the driveway, the back of it packed with garbage bags of clothes, boxes of photo albums, and perma-marked rows of nutrition books, and in the front seat was Mindi, smiling back at me.

PART III

THE STORK

Mino Bimaadiziwin

When I still lived at Westview Place, Mindi took me for a weekend boat trip to Big Chief Island with Chiclets and the rest of the good-lifers. It was dark out when she picked me up in Chiclets' Jeep, and like any good guests we made a stop at the Beer Store, which was connected to a sad Timmies that people got married at sometimes. Before pulling into a neighbourhood of cookie-cutters and McMansions, Mindi warned me that the friends we were visiting on Brewery Lane were wealthy and that I should be aware and on my best behaviour. At a certain point the houses started to hide behind massive trees and tall gates and epic shrubbery. Turns out the nicest houses in Sunshine City are also the shyest. Mindi pulled into a driveway marked by two boulders, and the driveway was smoother than the road. The Jeep's headlights beamed off a bumblebee-yellow Lamborghini, and I started to squirm in my seat. This was it.

One ding-dong and knock combo on the front door was all it took for me to see why Mindi was in such a hurry to get out of Happyland. I was hit with a lively gust of the good life. We were let inside by one of the hottest ladies Little Miss Dominion had to offer and led into a kitchen the size of unit 606 in its entirety. I sat on a barstool and bopped my head to the music while grown-up playboys boogied around me.

In the morning I woke up in one of the guest bedrooms and went down to the kitchen to find Mindi and the rest of them drinking Miller Genuine Draft and shooters and talking about Mindi's new nutrition practice, which she'd been developing for some time. Someone had driven the yellow Lambo to Timmies to pick up egg-cheese-and-bacon sandwiches for breakfast, much to Mindi's chagrin, but even she couldn't deny their exquisiteness. We spent the rest of the morning chilling and nice-housing, and then in the afternoon everyone decided it was time to take the boat out to Big Chief.

We hopped in and zoom-zoomed away from Brewery Lane until the dock was nothing but a red and pencil-thin mirage wub-wubbing in the distance. Chiclets focused on steering the boat over giant waves, which is probably tough enough when you're sotally tober. Our smiles widened and our whoas grew more audible with each wave, but then it got so loud that nobody could hear anything.

When we got to the inlet, Chiclets tossed the anchor off the back. *Cooper's Crib* had a stainless-steel fridge, a galley kitchen, and two bedrooms. They had so many toys on the floor deck that they called it Toyland. The Wiggles on the TV to keep the kids occupied while everybody else was outside Having Fun. It had a killer poop deck and a better poop bin than I ever pooped in. Even had a barbecue, like the ones people keep out in their backyard. Air smelled like latex, beer-can chicken, cold ones, and constipated dumps made up of pumpernickel loafs with ranch in the middle for double dipping. Plenty of canned diet pop for red cup mixes and shooters, scalding vinyl and burlap off old camping chairs, and ladies taking their tops off to show the bros their double Ds. They were nice.

There was a row of boats lined up on the other side of *Cooper's Crib*. On the boats were five, ten, maybe twenty playboys, plus us. Each of them shook hands with me and introduced themselves, names like Doug and Billy and Craig and Chiclets and Tim.

Mindi and Chiclets sat on the bow of the boat smooching and grooving and losing track of time. I had never seen grown-ups behave like this before, but I liked seeing Mindi so happy, rocking the new boob job and a Native Pride hat and fork-combed hair, just loving the heartbeat up in the sky. But no amount of boats or playboys or tequila sunrise or Big Chiefing would change the fact that we were just a couple of half-bads in white regalia.

So, I got up and brushed the wrinkles off my shorts, and even though there was no rostrum, I announced to everyone that I wanted a boat. *Cooper's Crib* woo-girled and fuck yeah'd and clinked their cups and cold ones. But it was Tim who took off his shades and spoke up. That's when everything went hush-hush.

"Why you want a boat?"

"Best way to the good life," I told him.

He laughed and sat up from his seat to cheers my can of Nestea and said abso-fuckin-lutely this is the good life all right.

"There's only one way to get a boat, kid," Tim said. "You gotta become an engineer."

"What's an engineer?"

Cooper's Crib erupted into giggles.

"Depends on what type of engineer you're talking about, son. There's all kinds. I'm a construction engineer, Doug over here is in computers. Craig is in logistics, so he's like an engineer for loans. Point is, we make things run smooth. It's no easy work. But at least it leads to a boat and a salary. Keeps you living the good life."

So it was settled. I was going to grow up and become an engineer. It didn't matter that I was no good at math without a calculator or that I didn't know how to tie shoes yet or that *engineer* was just a word to me. It was the good life that I understood. I wanted in.

Thelma and Louise

September swept in with Mindi's plan for a fresh start and an uneven First Choice bowl-cut. She was still with Chiclets, but when he wasn't at Cobblestone Cottage he was living in Toronto for work. Mindi, Iggy, and I moved to Barrie, where we split the den in a basement apartment we rented from a faux redhead in her thirties, who staged the only couch in the apartment with twenty-dollar HomeSense pillows I was told not to touch, who tossed our jackets, shoes, and any evidence of us on our floor when she hosted dinner parties, who taught me how to scramble eggs, who asked if something was burning when she farted next to us on our blow-up mattress.

Mindi and I couldn't stand the redhead, so we spent our days at viewings in downtown Barrie and at the library, geeking out about anything from the evils of margarine to the miracle of probiotics to holistic approaches to living and thriving off the land. I researched everything I could about crested geckos and pirates and dragons and magic tricks, which made me think I was one step closer to discovering the sublunary slippages between this world and the next. But I never got there.

Come December, Mindi and I briefly stayed with Auntie Meesh, whose McMansion had imploded with a cold separation that took wind out of her marketing company's six-figure-plus success and left her eating Swiss Chalet rotisserie and Wendy's chili in her bathrobe. Mindi and Meesh had raised their eldest kids together in Toronto in the nineties, intertwining their pains, their park and beach days, so tight they called each other Thelma and Louise. Two of them kicked ass, babes to boot. After some twenty-plus years of putting up with the hair-thinning Bullshit of Men, they were both free. Must have felt like relighting the beacons of Gondor, like filling a chainsaw hole with wood shavings. Thelma had recently finished nutrition school. Louise was newly single and ready to take that six-figure salary back. So after years of prep and school and enough rent for an apartment of one's own, Thelma drove off the cliff with her homegirl and moved to Midland to open up her first-ever practice, with the goal to flush as many digestive systems in town as she could. The momentum injected them with enough gusto to hop out the storm drain they dropped in nearly twenty years back. They even brought me and Iggy along with them.

On a sunny day in December, our U-Haul pulled up to a slippery crooked staircase that led to a red door that led to a two-storey apartment. Aside from a wooden table with smooth drawers and no more than a room's worth of decor Thelma had kept since the divorce, we didn't have much furniture (much of it either left in

Happyland or locked in some musty, inaccessible storage unit in downtown Sunshine City), so the three of us took turns booting ice chunks off the stairs and loading Louise's furniture into the house. Steel floor lights, oak mantelpieces, a secretary desk, a box television, two purple leather couches, a surround sound from her basement, an Olympic mattress, and a Dell slowly made their way through the foyer. My possessions amounted to a few books, two band posters, and a bonsai, which I decided to keep next to the bathtub, since it grew best near wetness and humidity.

I started going to a new school, where I didn't have many friends, mind one bratty kid who reviewed his mother's PlentyofFish profile and called her out for using old pictures. After coming over and seeing our house-in-development, he took up the habit of waiting until a certain quartet of cute girls in our class were around to gesture at me and say "Cody doesn't even have a friggin' bed," a problem Thelma solved with the Barrie blow-up mattress, which I liked sleeping on anyways.

Near December's end, Julian and Kris came to visit from Sunshine City. Kris had also left Adam and Eve's and she'd moved into Debbie's spare room after O Touro went back into rehab. Julian swiftly followed after Dyson's chain-smoking, vehemently Catholic mom kicked him out cuz her boyfriend came home drunk after losing a bunch of money at the casino and tried to pick a fight with Dyson. So Julian put him in a headlock until he passed out. He wasn't allowed to stay after that.

It had taken Kris months of paycheques to save up enough for her own place, and she could finally afford first and last. Nobody would rent to her and Julian at first, but they finally found a two-bedroom on Coldwater Road. They left Debbie's spare after a stupid fight and hid together in the new apartment's attic for a few days. After their move-in date, they filled the space with the remaining furniture from Westview, most of which had been left behind to must in storage.

That evening we went to a party at Thelma's wellness centre. Us three kids sat in her new office, which she decorated with no more than a couple Bio-K sample trays, a huge blond-stained wood table that survived from storage, and a schmancy bookshelf full of old and new tomes. We had our best shirts on, smiling at those folks knocking back wine, endless go-getters filing like ants in and out of Thelma's office for a sample, a pamphlet, and a complimentary consultation.

Mindi and I spent that Christmas at Chiclets' parents place on Brewery Lane. They had the second biggest house on the street, and when we walked inside, the ultra-clean rooms turned labyrinthine. I slid across the buffed hardwood and listened to rich good-lifers spit wisdom and high-brow silliness. We ate soft-boiled eggs in ceramic cups with blue glaze, and I brought the best behaviour I had. I slept on a bed with a hundred pillows that came out to the middle of it and just slept on them like that, not wanting to wreck the comfy.

O Touro's Boy

Fresh out of rehab, O Touro drove us past patches of countryside in a brand-new rental. Small store-blocks went by. Fuzzy Rock 95 commercials screamed winter-tire deals at us, but the snow had yet to fall.

Bachelor flats and trash white-panel houses lined the fronts of shuffling backdrops that occasionally bounced out of frame with little bumps or potholes. Sold to those working for a mortgage in the Harper era, an era of I-told-you-sos. Out on the highway, some houses were lucky enough to have a veranda or an enclosed porch, and the houses that had one always used it for junk and scrap. The highway stretches of stores popped whenever you took in the long ranges of dead off-season dirt around them. None of these corners had much a twelve-year-old like me would have liked much, mind stale porno mags that grew dusty, sterile, and colourless on the back shelves of corner gas plazas, between lumber yards and the like. We stopped for gas and a pack and to cash in a winning twelve-dollar ticket and I'd watch O Touro flip to the last page of the *Toronto Sun*, consider it, let the ink stain his fingertips, and shuffle me back into the car with a bag of Doritos, which I just know had more heft and chips back then.

We drove past transporters that farted trails of poisonous cloud and raced down lanes and honked honks that touched your lungs when you'd least expect a good honk and I felt sorrow for those men who knew about living life like O Touro, a Hydro One vet with the odd weekend off. Over ten years of taking chainsaws to ancient logs along empty stretches to make way for money-making power lines owned by Hydro, only to have the government privatize the company and bust the union a few years later. Men who carved a way for Little Miss Dominion. How fast could O Touro pump the brakes if one of the car-carrier trailer fuses took a power-trip, or a wheel went over an unseen pothole?

We headed farther down Highway 11 and it went smooth for a bit and I could thank the workers for that. O Touro adjusted his hat. I had never been to Oro, which is where he said we were headed for the weekend. I only saw it on maps and in my periphery when visiting O Touro's other apartments, dens, and temporaries. But our schedules aligned and that was that.

He coughed little bits of his tarry self into his sleeve and we took turns answering each other's questions. Mine to keep him from asking his, and his characterized by a need to tackle the two Ms: Mindi and money. Hydro One usually laid him off for the winter, so I sat as far back into the seat as I could and made the most of the freeway views.

"How's your new place?" I asked.

"It's good for now, in a trailer. Got a TV."

"A trailer?"

"Just for a bit. Telling you."

Without asking, Ontario flipped the snow switch on us, and rows of flakes floated upon and beyond the brand-new rental.

"It's snowing."

"Oh good. Yup." He kept his foot on the wheel and switched on the wipers and turned the heat up high. We continued through silt roads until we entered a lot of trailers. We stopped at the last one, at the very end, and Hydro One workers and park friends came inside and drank and called me a good boy. I think they just called me boy. O Touro's boy.

Like Ice Cream the Scoop Can't Fit

Come February, Midland's ill chill temps could nip fingertips and caress the neck moments after leaving the mudroom, so Thelma whipped up batches of beef barley soup. Recipe made enough to last for at least a week, depending on what crockpot you got and how many people need to eat. Beef barley's long-term benefits counterbalanced Thelma's early struggle keeping clients, often potato-shaped one-offs bent on keeping their insides backed up. So to help make the stretch to the month's end, she got a part-time job at a crab shack, with Louise joining shortly thereafter.

Thelma and I took grocery trips together for organic butter, Kashi cereal, and Dimpflmeier ("Any ethical registered nutritionist would never feed her own son poison! Nuh-uh-uh, sorry babe!") and went to nautical-themed restaurants you had to enter through the back door in order to be seated. When I packed a lunch, fellow classmates took a few minutes to pass around the freakazoid healthy alternatives I brought, so I learned that it was best to wait for the walk home to enjoy the seed bread sandwiches and soybean solutions. When the recess bell forced us out into the day's blizzard, I made my way to the school field's corner, where exposed bits of skin got whipped with wind, stood, and waited for the bell's ding. Our first and only winter in Midland ended with Chiclets' Jeep getting the stereo ripped out one night and a case of pneumonia for me. I spent plenty of days at the office with Thelma, who would praise me for the patience I showed when I waited for her to finish up with a client, but I told her it was no biggie.

At the onset of the summer, we took an overnighter to Algonquin on *Cooper's Crib*, splashing through a canal into the back half of the lock, sunshine everywhere except in our eyes. All around were massive cliffs with rock-rooted trees leaning over them, doming the river like a fish-eye lens. The evening light gave the place a movie-set feel and gave the endless tunnel of still, emerald freshwater our boats bloop-blooped and vroomed through a seamless peeling, like ice cream the scoop can't fit. Thelma bid me off with their friend who loved Stella Artois so much he named his dog after it and who loved me so much I got to steer his boat for a moment, too blitzed in feeling dangerous like how Akon sang it through the radio to notice how easily Thelma let me go, instead of anxiously, like the hot-dog-cutter from Happyland she was. We docked at a rock cliff with a trashed fire pit at the bottom of it. Everybody began drinking shortly after *Cooper's Crib* fought with another yacht for anchor room cuz their boats were too huge. The go-to line for the rest of the night was "You're in my swing space, buddy," which the speaker followed with the swinging of their pelvis. Hours of this went on and then Thelma took me to the edge of the cliff to dangle our feet, with the twinkling dark above us. She began tearing up a little and asked if I wanted another sibling. I asked her if she was pregnant and she said she wasn't but was saying it cuz I want you to have one, baby. Would be kinda nice, a little sibling, don't you think?

"But I already have two."

"No worries, just forget I said anything then, babe . . ."

One month later, Thelma amicably split with Chiclets and, in an awkward switch, fell for his nephew JD, a suntanned diabetic. Mindi had gone from Chiclets' girl to Thelma at the edge of the cliff. Except the cliff was just a porch she was smoking on in the early morning, watching the dew form and the early fog stew in the blue muted light.

Constipation Blues

In a whirring white Ford, Thelma, her twenty-seven-year-old boyfriend, JD, JD's West Coast Tahltan pal Jaybird, and twelve-year-old me whipped down Highway 11 to Sunshine City.

I was spending a much-needed week at Kris and Julian's place on Coldwater Road, where I could pull all-nighters playing *Halo 2* co-op with Julian and watch their endless supply of burnt DVDs. I cycled through recent Facebook messages about the fun we'd have while riding in the back seat next to an open two-four of Miller.

We hit downtown and pulled up to a house with a FOR RENT sign in the front window. Westview Place was just uphill, two stoplights away. Kris and Julian's apartment was a short turn down Coldwater Road, at the bottom of a parking lot for a funeral home. But first we had to stop at JD's friend Lee's townhouse. I followed Thelma single-file through the darkness to a side door.

"Yo son, what's good with you? Welcome to the crib." We walked in and shook Lee's hand.

"Excuse me, can I use the washroom, please?" I asked.

A guy at a table rolling a Zig-Zag waved me over and pointed: "Down that hallway to the kitchen, then take a right."

I entered the bathroom and felt the wall for a light switch. A bare bulb flickered in sync with a vent-fan I was thankful for. Hated when people heard me in the washroom. I hadn't shit for two days in a row that week. And when it came, food barely left the stomach: the gastric motel for last week's barley soup and slices from Papas Pizza. My obstructed intestinal tract slowed down when Thelma resigned her office space and had to leave the wellness centre and work full-time at the crab shack.

I squeezed stomach muscles and glanced at the few arrivals floating in the toilet. I dropped pieces of toilet paper in fear of a second pair of eyes and flushed. Left the bathroom still feeling like I had to go.

I pulled up my baggy pants and wandered toward the noise. Found a dank room with stains on the carpet. Lights dim as hell. Mismatched couches. Shithole must have been the living room. A dusty second-gen PlayStation 2 and a Super Nintendo were in one corner, and the same guy rolling the same joint sat in the other. A *Guitar Hero II* song menu looped on an out-of-place big screen. On the coffee table, a Budweiser with a cigarette floating lonely.

"Hey, babe, out here."

I walked out to the balcony and found Thelma, Jaybird, JD, and Lee laughing and holding Millers, chatting about the night ahead. JD and Lee were red in the face and sweaty, like they just ran the Terry Fox. Thelma's silhouette cast against colourful stacks of beer cases and mismatched brick. I counted the empties like brown tokens for dimes and coveted Lee's sweet collection. Beat what little empties I kept in the backyard, saving up for an Xbox 360.

Thelma had a beer-smoke combo in her hand and kept telling Jaybird and me how much fun this was. She told me it was almost time they cut for the KEE to Bala, a country bar out in Muskoka.

"We got to go real soon, baby. The Hip's going on in an hour!"

"But Kris isn't home from work yet." I'd phoned her three times to no answer.

"Babe, we'll miss the Hip if we don't leave in five or so."

One by one we walked out of Lee's trap. Thelma, JD, and Jaybird chugged on the drive to Kris and Julian's apartment. We took two rights and pulled into a tenant parking lot beside a townhouse, the funeral home just beyond it. I grabbed my backpack and shut the door.

After sending missed calls and a slurry voicemail to Kris's cellphone, plus some boozestorming, JD decided to spider his way up and along the apartment roof. He whipped out a pocket knife I'd never seen before, slashed through the upstairs window screen of Kris's apartment, then disappeared into the hole. Thelma and Jaybird cheered him from the gravel driveway.

"Nice job, baby!"

"Fucking right! Way to go, man!"

Within a minute, JD unlocked the apartment door and shoved his knife-holding fist into the Sunshine City night, channelling a breezy wind running along the streetlights of Coldwater Road. Thelma kissed me on the forehead and hugged me over the shoulders.

"I'm leaving my phone with you. I'll come get it tomorrow. Enjoy your break, baby. I love you more than you know."

"Love you, too."

They waved goodbye, and JD's Ford took off before I shut the door.

Inside Kris's place, I summoned the best robber I had in me, tiptoeing my way through. I turned on a bathroom light, illuminating a framed swan print that had made it from the house in Happyland's dining room. To the left of the bathroom was Kris's room. I opened her door. She had her furniture synthesized with the tangerine walls and her jewellery laid on top of a fireplace mantel. Four bay windows, through which light would come blasting in the morning. A green bong called Hulk, which she used to keep tucked away in her bedroom closet back at Westview, now stood proudly plunked on a table in front of curtains that blew with the wind. The faint leftover bongstink jogged a brain pic of Kris paying in advance for a tree from the West Ridge Home Depot so that Julian and I could have Christmas. And then another one of Julian and me playing Muchachi's Xbox and his copy of OG *Halo* all night, five nights in a row. Sometimes even four-player with Kris and Muchachi, too. The television setup looked only slightly overcrowded, the surround sound's messy wiring tucked behind.

I felt my way along the walls to a kitchen painted intestinal red, where I found cupboards packed with snacks for the week. Rock-hard green bananas, three milk bags, a new loaf of Dempster's. Coffee mugs hung from little hooks above the empty sink, glossy black dishes and cutlery still wet in the drying rack. House shit

Kris had paid in advance and collected for years. For our very own nice house.

After the kitchen, I stopped at a set of stairs with chipped paint steps that split two walls fading up a chasm and into black. Band posters, *Revolver* magazine cutouts, and rows of New Era brims caked the wall. I took out the knock-off fitted I found in a Goodwill and raised it next to Julian's hats. The night robber in me butterflied into a little brother entering the much cooler older brother's room. The white bulb of an Ikea lamp standing at the top of the steps revealed JD's slice through the window screen. Stacks of CDs and burnt discs sat on top of Julian's old dresser, our names still carved on the side. Albums Julian used to play at O Touro's apartment piled high in two columns: AOF, System, Billy T, Ozzy, and more—even some new ones he'd play for me tomorrow. "Listen to this," Julian would say when he blasted the stereo. "Better than that Fall Out Boy crap. Why you listen to that anyways?"

Back downstairs was the open-concept living room. A great big space with the leftover spirit of my siblings in it. Walls painted the colour of sage. My sister had positioned the two bookshelves that came with Julian's old bunk bed on each side of The Plasma. Both shelves were full of DVDs and Xbox games. Photos of us three on her computer desk and a wad of hundreds poking out an envelope on The Plasma. Most of the stuff I recognized had survived Westview and Happyland. Whatever endured and kept returning. That potted tree that was a couple years older than me still chilling in the corner of the study. All quiet mind the wind running.

I turned on The Plasma and powered up the Xbox right away. The furniture confirmed a hole by filling one. I thought about the old Rogers box and how even after it bunked, Julian and I discovered we could take turns sticking our thumbs into the end of the cable cord for reception, creating a fuzzy connection for dinnertime *Simpsons* reruns. I'd watch for his reactions and laugh whenever he laughed until he told me to stop copying him, to laugh when I wanted to laugh. We had a Rogers box in Westview too, but that was before the night the cops came and Theresa from Child Services pulled me from class to ask pointed questions about quality of life. Whatever that was.

Thelma's pay-as-you-go Telus vibrated off the desk and onto the laminate. It kept vibrating. No caller ID.

I picked up. "Hello?"

"Mom, don't you . . . Cody? Where's Mom?" Kris asked.

I inhaled for another one of her level 99+ yellfights. "I'm at your house. She went to the KEE to Bala."

"What the hell? How did you get in?"

"JD climbed the apartment and cut the window."

"Cut the window? The fucking window . . . You gotta go, Cody. I'm sorry. Right now. Go."

"But they already left Lee's for the KEE. There's nowhere to go."

"Then go back there right now. I swear to God I'm gonna kill her. What a shit mother. I have to get back to work. She's not just dropping you off like that."

I was at the door by the time the call was over. I hoped Master Chief from *Halo* was waiting on the other side of it, energy sword in hand to release at least half the nerves I had and take me on a mission to finally finish the fight on the ring. Outside everything was quiet, mind the wind and a few siren wails coming from around the waterfront on the other side of Sunshine City. I ran to the intersection panicking, and with nowhere to go, knocked on Lee's door. He opened it and gave me a hug, told me they were just about to leave so I better hurry. I found Thelma sitting on the couch. Her face flipped like inverted controls when she saw me. After five minutes, her Telus began vibrating and she hit speaker.

"What is wrong with you, Mom? Not sober enough to watch Cody for a few fucking hours? Soon as you feel like it you drop him off? So you can party with your cokehead loser boyfriend and his buddies? Who also by the way are my age? One of these days, I'll take you to court and take Cody back. Just you wait."

They didn't end up going to see the Hip, and instead spent the rest of the night hanging out in the living room. My planned week with Kris and Julian was cancelled.

On the way home to Midland, Thelma, JD, and Jaybird sped down the highway blasting Bon Jovi. When we were about halfway there, JD's rearview mirror filled up with flashes. They scrambled to kick the empties under their seats. At four in the morning, a cruiser pulled over a car full of drunkos and a twelve-year-old half-bad with an open can of Canada Dry in the back, whose stomach still felt full of crap.

Where the Cougars Went

O Touro came to pick us up from the DUI. After that he stayed in Midland with us for a week or two. He and Thelma weren't smooching or sleeping in the same room or anything like that, but they were hanging out and drinking and laughing together, which was spooky enough.

On his first night in Midland, O Touro found me struggling to fall asleep on Louise's sticky purple leather couch while a particularly wild party raged on across the street, so he walked over and kicked butt in his construction boots. Thelma always told me she was only thankful for O Touro cuz he gave her us kids and could beat anybody up if needed.

JD and Jaybird had started living at the house. Those days got so barnyard hot you couldn't get to the Brita filter fast enough. Jaybird spent his spare time on the purple leather loveseat, pointing his lips at the foldout of Rihanna's *Good Girl Gone Bad* CD and staring endlessly ("Now that's a beautiful, REAL woman, eh Cody? Holee!"). He wasn't wrong.

Thelma and Louise got into plenty fighting and door slamming, and after sleeping in from a night of Coronas in bathrobes, Michael Bublé covers skipping in the kitchen stereo, I'd watch Louise spoon saucy pasta from a caked pot on the stove into Chow-Chow's food bowl in the mudroom. Don't blame her. Best she could do between stealing Thelma's shifts at the crab shack and her new serving job at the golf resort. Chow-Chow didn't eat it, so the foyer maggots did.

During the hot, clammy middays of Midland, Thelma and Louise sat in the kitchen or at our weeded backyard patio table, our daily walk-in pizzas for a slice of good life. But then came the toe-cutting brown bottles crunching against the kitchen floor, which were always syncing with the chorus of bosses and monsters I would slay in *Fable*, until the long-desired horns sprouted out the hero's bald spots and his eyes went yellowish. Around midnight, Louise would come stumbling to her Dell beside the mudroom to blast one of her tunes, and before I knew it, Timbaland's fat-belly and vocoded boom was spanking the floor, talk to me girl. She would often come up to me shlammered, shaking her ass around the house, filling it up with herself. I was so embarrassed by those songs that I began running upstairs on a knee jerk.

One evening in the living room, when it was just us two, O Touro asked me turn off *Splinter Cell* and told me to listen up cuz he was telling me. And then it came.

"I need to borrow your money, bud."

I wanted an Xbox 360 that year so I could play *Halo 3* with Julian when it came out in the fall. I went looking for a job until Mindi introduced me to the handyman living across the street. During the day, the handyman would hand me his beat-up and grass-stained mower and point to the end of a stranger's yard, where I'd cut everything overgrown, the mulching blade whizzing stone pebbles and weeds at both shin bones. I kept every dollar I made from the yards and the empties and celebrated with ice cream when I reached two hundred. At that point I began carrying the savings on me, folding the twenties, arranging them in order of fresh to least, ironing them, laying them out side by side. I reminded O Touro about the Xbox 360.

"Look, Cody. I know you're saving for an X-pee, but I don't have any way out of here. Don't you care about that? I'm near homeless, all right? In a real slump. Worst it's ever been. Don't you care about that? Don't you care about me?"

And so I gave him the money. In the morning, O Touro's construction boots were gone, and this once-in-a-while was officially over.

I could hear Thelma calling for me from upstairs. Cody, c'mon up babe it's a brand-new day. She'd gone out the night before with Louise, which explained the homie snoring on the other purple leather couch.

Out in the back, Louise sat down in her bathrobe, Bic-ing a smoke. A few nights before that, she'd started getting a little physical with me when she drank. Stomps here, little shoves there. When I told her to bug off for getting in my face during a *Fable* boss fight, she pushed me headfirst into her purple couch, asking

"What? You claustrophobic, Cody? What's that? Can't hear you, babe!" Don't think she'd remember this if you asked her about it today. Don't think she'd remember the homie trying to get his dick wet who got locked out the house one night when she took off to get pizza. I sat with him in the weeded backyard and watched the heartbeat come up, pointed him in the wrong way when he asked where the cougars went, yup, that's the best way to find one, saw hundreds on the prowl, waiting in the orchards and cedars.

Thelma kept calling for me, so I blackened both feet on the stairs to her and she gave me a kiss and told me about her night. She asked if she could borrow a twenny for a pack of cigs and promised to pay me back after her shift, but when I told her why I couldn't give her any money, she got a stern look on her face. "Thought I taught you better than to give him that money. Hope you know you won't be getting it back." Her voice got serious as she started to tell me about O Touro's Problem, even though I already knew and jeez get over it already.

In July we took off to Christian Island for a weekend, JD and Thelma looking real cheesed trying to find me a place to sleep for the night so they could party around a rez tent with some neechie playboys. The next morning they picked me up, my backpack stuffed with PlayStation 2 games lifted from the boy whose parents agreed to watch me, JD hunched over and spitting in the sand cuz his insulin pump had run out and Thelma with a new turtle necklace drooped down her clavicle and a spirit name from one horny local. We made our way through the heated, exhausted men crowding the ferry terminal, mostly Nishfolk and chinstrap fellas who lived on the island, and set off on foot until we could find a ride to hitch. Made it to the blue sign for Midland before we realized we were heading the wrong way. We sweated down those backroads, Thelma and Jaybird desperately jerking their thumbs into the air every time a car drove by, JD's sweat yellowing the white of his wife-beater, until a Volkswagen Beetle finally stopped. We hopped into the back, where bags from a fresh grocery run crowded our feet. I sat in the middle and watched Jaybird bend over next to me, squishing pieces of bread into his fist with a subtle giggle, nibbling on it, still blitzed.

In August, I had to sell Iggy cuz of the crickets cricketing in the floor vents, chirping after everybody left for another party, passed out on the sofas, or whenever I went to make midnight cucumber sandwiches in the kitchen. You could hear those chirps in the foyer, in the bathroom, in Thelma's vitamin closet. Louise said they were making Chow-Chow sick, and all of us living in the house at that point generally agreed nobody could take another cricket if they saw one. When we dropped Iggy off at the pet food store, the cashier told us he had the gecko equivalent of bone cancer and was basically unsellable. Said crested geckos needed way more than these Midland crickets and it's a good thing we brought him in when we did.

By the end of that month, the bonsai had completely dried up beside the bathtub and a SWAT team went and busted the neighbours next door, raining on some poor fella's trip, bringing the whole neighbourhood and local news to gather around the bottom of our porch steps. During the hotter days, I'd sit with Thelma and Louise at the dinner table or out back, either in their bathrobes or catching bra strap and farmer tans, thumbing limes into their Coronas, du Maurier smoke floating around the bottle necks, debating whose kids were hungrier and yapping up the very genuine regrets that only two half-bads could have in their forties. Louise told Thelma she got everything in life handed to her cuz she was born with a feather in her hair. And when it was just us two, Thelma would tell me how her father died, how she found him, and everything seemed to shift in a way I didn't like.

One night I heard the red door slam, and from my bedroom window I watched Louise stumble across the road to the soft glow of the neighbour's porch light. I went downstairs and found Thelma sitting on the arm of one of the purple leather couches, putting on a Train CD.

"You okay if I play one, babe? Just a song? Won't be long."

"That's fine with me, Mom."

The two of us listened to it and she began singing and crying at the same time and then I knew she was thinking about the stork again.

The Stork

Nana Maggie spent six months in one of those schools. Little is known about her parents, except that her father was a farmer and her mother died alone in a hotel. A family in Fairford took her in and raised her on the rez. But they couldn't stop Reverend Cowley and other black coats from knocking at their door, looking for kids from the Partridge Crop to fit onto that bus.

Records show that most children who attended were not allowed to cry after they arrived. And when a child can't cry, that cry can stay inside and hide for a long time. That cry will make its way into the organs and brain pics and into the amygdala and make scrambled eggs of the senses.

Back then, you didn't want to get registered. Back then, you didn't want that little card. Back then, Nana Maggie didn't want to live on the rez, was just a nineteen-year-old who worked as a nanny. A single mother stuck on flight mode, she had to plan Mindimooye's adoption before she left the womb. Praying that her baby wouldn't end up at one of those schools, she'd caught wind of the scoop and made her way to Toronto for the placement.

"When a child is adopted on exit, they get certain messages when in utero," Mindimooye tells me. "So what happens when your mother's pregnant with you and she's starving herself? Or she's been drinking? Or she's only nineteen? My birth mom drank with every one of her three kids and she never ate. Most babies who come out like that are obese. Don't forget about the diabetes. Why? Because they get these physiological messages that teach them how to retain things. And then they eat Wonder Bread. No wonder."

Little Miss Dominion gave Maggie no choice, told her that Mindimooye would be raised Catholic under the adoption agreement. Even found the right couple to do it: the Millians. But of course, this being a half-bad story, plans changed at the last minute. Cuz the Millian couple were friends with another couple, one with a major case of baby fever.

Nana Flo's husband, Charles, emigrated from Malta and was the first of his immediate family to make it to Little Miss Dominion. Charles was the kind of patriot who lied to get himself enlisted and joined the air force when he was thirteen years old. Before he could even drive a car he was parachuting out of planes. There are pictures of him in his paratrooper outfit sitting in Mindimooye's basement somewhere.

Charles came back from the war with bigwig plans to start a limousine business. A couple years after their first son was born, he told Flo he wanted another one. Just one. And then he heard that their friend Dorothy Millian was on the wait-list for the baby placement program. Charles insisted, said if Dorothy Millian is doing it then why couldn't we? Nana Flo objected, reminded him that she'd happily cut her ovaries out after the second pregnancy permafried them, told him she didn't need another newborn around the house, let alone a daughter at that. But Charles didn't quit pestering and made her go anyways.

In the spring of 1964, Nana Flo and Charles met the Millians at the hospital in the nearly empty eastern wing of ICUs. At one end was the Millian-to-be baby in an incubator and her mother, who'd given birth few days before. At the other end was Nana Maggie, nineteen going on twenty, who'd popped out Mindimooye at four in the morning. Nana Maggie wouldn't leave the wing until she knew who was taking Mindimooye, whom the nurses immediately took away after the birth.

Both couples paid for their respective babies with cash. The DeGiorgios adopted Mindimooye for fifteen bucks. Charles put her in his working cab and him and Flo took her home to their Scarborough bungalow. The doctor who came to check up on her drove a Jaguar and wore a plush esiban coat. He thought Mindimooye was better off not knowing her real family, and the neighbours agreed. They reminded Flo to "treat a brown-skinner like one." People asked them where the baby was from, cuz it sure as hell wasn't Toronto. They always said she came from the stork.

A year or two after the stork came, Charles's limousine business hit it big. He got lucky and scored a contract for a private airport on the north end of the city. Anybody who flew in on a private jet got driven to their gig by his company. Not to mention there were only two other limo services in the city at the time. So in the back seat would be Mark Hamill or Deborah Kerr or Ringo Starr and sitting there in shotgun was wee Mindimooye.

"As far back as I remember, Nana Flo was always pissed at me. Especially because Charles wasn't a great man to her. If she pissed me off, I used to go tell him and he'd give her a backhand. If the pasta wasn't right, he'd whip his bowl across the room.

"One of my first memories is knowing that my favourite person in the world has to leave me. I remember someone knocking on the front door. And when Nana Flo opens it I look through her legs and see my father standing on our porch. His cab is at the curb, running. One of his girlfriends is sitting in shotgun. I just lose it: I'm so happy to see him and his cab, the cab light, one of those little lights that light up white and go ding ding ding.

"Nana Flo is standing between us two, screaming at him 'I told you I never wanted to be stuck with this! I didn't want to have to deal with this!' And I know right away who *this* is. He turns away and starts to leave. I start screaming 'Daddy! Daddy! Please don't go!'

"But he keeps standing on that porch. 'Let me see my little girl. C'mon, Flo. Let me see her.' I can hear this line over and over in my head all the time."

When Mindimooye was old enough to walk outside and look up at the sky, people stared at her like she had six heads on. At Catholic school she got this six heads crap before, during, and after class. At home, her brother told her that her real mom was a bearded lady wrestler who was black, too. And so one day on the patio swing she asked her dad where she came from.

"The first thing I'm ever told is that the stork dropped me off in a picnic basket on the lawn. Imagine that the first thing you were ever told is that the stork dropped you off in a picnic basket on the lawn. That nobody here or anywhere near here is your real family. And to then grow up with that feeling and not know what's going on until half your life has gone by. That's why you and your siblings stayed in that situation for so long. I didn't want to have my own children feel like I felt that day. No matter what. Everything that happened to me turned me into the person I am. But at the end of the day, I'm still that baby on my dad's front lawn."

When she was ten, Mindimooye was home alone and burned the house down trying to cook some food for herself. They moved into the Hilton Hotel at the airport, much to Flo's chagrin. After six months in the hotel, they moved back into their renovated Downsview house, which the insurance paid to repair. Mindimooye transferred schools again and switched to a private girls' institution, complete with measured uniforms and invoiced tuition. Intimidating and prim Italians who had hope chests in their bedrooms and boyfriends to kiss come lunchtime would attack her, push her down, or pants her in front of the school bus. Got mad enough to beat the worst one up. But no matter what, everybody bugged her about that stork basket. Asking how it made her feel.

She started pretending she was Italian, French, Maltese, whatever she felt like that day. Trouble came when she finally made friends and started exploring the city with them, sneaking vodka orange juices and unbuckling their belts for the little think. Mindimooye hadn't even got her period yet, but got a handle on partying, accidentally overdosing after she turned fifteen, and waking up plenty on the apartment floor.

Not long after that, Charles and Nana Flo broke up for good and Mindimooye moved into an apartment in Toronto with Charles. One day when she was sixteen, she woke up on the apartment floor cuz the phone was ringing over and over. It was Flo, and what could she possibly want?

"Where is he? He's got six runs here waiting for him."

"Let him sleep, Ma, he's been complaining," she said. "Gonna need another driver today."

A few hours later she called again. "Go shake him. He needs to pick people up. Don't hang up until you wake him."

It was then that Mindimooye got a weird feeling. She ran to her father to wake him. Blood from deep inside him bubbled out his mouth. She grasped his arm and shook it over and over. Ran back to her dangling phone call with Flo. Flo told her to shake him.

Mindimooye left bruises all over his arms. Then the landlord and the officers came. They all told her to leave but she didn't until the coroner came in and pronounced him dead. They didn't let her back in for the rest of the day.

There were so many people at the funeral that there was only room to stand. At the wake, Mindimooye remembers hearing an auntie crap-talking Charles for hitting Nana Flo. The auntie went on and on and then after a drink or two Mindimooye had had enough. A few of Charles's best men had to drag her away, her heels swinging in the parlour.

The funeral unglued Mindimooye. She dropped out of school and began to work full-time as a receptionist, work she knew how to do from helping out at her dad's office. On her days off she'd go for a perm, let the dresser stick rods through her hair and fix it with a pick to fluff up her curls. Everybody got a perm back then.

Mindimooye's brother moved in with her and stayed for two years, until he fell in love and got married. So Mindimooye decided to move back in with Nana Flo and then eventually into the apartment next door so they could both have some space. She began to go out more often to take her mind off the hum of not knowing what was up. She spent more time at bars that featured live music, like the Gasworks and Connections, the latter of which is where she met you-know-who.

"You don't realize the impact you can have on others, let alone your family. You do the best you can. The first thing that should've happened was going to counselling. But all those feelings of abandonment kept me from going. I'm not excusing myself, but God . . . I wish I could have gone to counselling back then. I wish I kept going to school. Sometimes I make wrong choices, Cody. But I can't change them. I can only change today."

Porno

Thelma began talking nonsense on our crooked porch steps about moving to British Columbia with JD. It began with that brooding people do when no one's around to watch them, shaking their cig and whispering, fucking dump this place is, plus other stuff to make a kid take in the sunset crowning the crack den across the street and think geez, this ain't no Happyland.

Gone was Chiclets and his leased Jeep that Thelma wheeled proudly. Gone was the two-finger wheel salute that made her smile fireworks for days. Gone was Thelma's nutrition practice that dangled the varied carrots of class mobility in front of us. Gone were wholesome thoughts of reuniting with Julian and Kris and buying back our Happyland house before it cursed the next set of owners with the stomp of divorce or the endless bang of needed repairs. Gone were schmancy orange roughy dinners and the effort it took to cook beef barley stew, something good steaming our wintry Midland windows with a warm, Christmas special glow.

Missed garbage day maggots overtook the Midland mudroom. Lines of squirmy-crawlies marched aimless around the dog bowls and runners, runners I stopped wearing when the blisters and warts appeared on both feet, to greet me when I stormed from the cig cloud growing thick in the porch humidity, thinking what the fuck us two were going to do in British Columbia.

Moving would also mean losing newfound freedom: freedom to get away from the house until after dark to meet neighbourhood kids and goof off near our foreclosed school; freedom to smack a plastic cup in a rage on the way upstairs so it could hit a day drunk in the foyer, despite aiming it at Louise, who carried herself like she still lived in her McMansion, even though she fed Chow-Chow leftover spaghetti. But above all, moving would mean losing a certain freedom I was only just beginning to discover. Yup. Porno.

JD and Jaybird had misplaced their *Girls Gone Wild* DVD a couple months back ("Funny, haven't seen anything . . ."), a mid-2000s edition they cheersed their beers to. When I gollumed the movie, slid it into an aquarium care manual on my black bookshelf, it introduced me to the most joyful of nerves, to the vibrant kitsch of purple whizzing rabbits between a lady's legs and muting the creepy camera-bro POV. I watched it almost daily after Thelma and the others left for downtown dives and our place got penny-drop quiet. I burned through it slow, edging at the thoughtcrimes these Girls gave me in one sweaty hand with a Hawaiian slice from Papas Pizza in the other. I risked watching in the living room no matter what time it was, especially when it wasn't a good time, like when they asked Tammy, a stick-thin, pimple-faced drifter who never left the neighbourhood, to watch me from six in the afternoon until the moon came out.

"I'll be out here if you need me, hun," Tammy said, Bic-ing a smoke and painting her toes, claiming post on our top step.

"But I don't need you." I backed away from the mudroom, toward the TV. "I'm twelve, you know."

"Well then, you let me know if you change your mind."

Even though Tammy's body scared me chickenshit and I pitied her for living in it, she was one of the sweetest people I met living there, gifting Dollar Store goodies when she stopped by our place to say hi and have a cig with Thelma. I even pictured having sex with her, but I wonder what guilt would have clung to me if I'd convinced a crackhead to mimic the Girls I watched from Louise's purple leather loveseat.

Instead I dreamt giddy about classmates or the girl from across the street who smiled and winked at me on the days I cut lawns for her pops, which I forgot about when he said she's sixteen and keep those eyes on the mower, brother. After I whirlwinded with the Taz-devils of puberty, I got hazy thinking how doomed my twelveness made me, so I took scissors to JD's *Hustler* stash and cut from it in clean strips.

I'd learned how to jerk off a couple years earlier. Video clips I downloaded off LimeWire and a hasty Google search for "porn" that I couldn't scrub from the computer. Haunted me for weeks, especially whenever my brother would ask to get into my account. I tried typing a bunch of similar searches ("nrop," "ponrope," "portable classrooms," "pork," "Pokemon") to cover it up, but the original baddie sin still laid in plain sight. Worst part was that nothing came up in the search except for some shitty illustrations. Total waste. I laid on the rugburn-blue Westview carpet with me and my boyhood facing the cottage-cheese ceiling and went at it like Portnoy. And then I came.

I flipped out for weeks over this untapped resource. I always knew that sex was something else, but now I could literally see what the else was. I started going to the toilet when I didn't need to use it, showering every day. I unearthed sex in everything.

So when I saw JD and Jaybird watching *Girls Gone Wild* I knew what I had to do.

With a red Solo cup in one hand, a sweaty and horny JD popped the disc in with the other, fingerprinting it. The steamy ballroom music filled our living room and the squealing came in hot. But I ran upstairs cuz I couldn't handle it. I was so angry that those idiots thought they could just put it on without anybody's permission, but extra angry that Thelma was too busy blasting Michael Bublé's cover album with Tammy in the kitchen to notice.

Eventually I found a chance to snatch it. Thelma and Louise and Jaybird and JD and others began opening up the Coronas and Thelma and Louise went off to do their makeup. As evening arrived, I went into the kitchen.

"Cody!" Louise said. "What the hell is taking her so long? Go tell her to hurry her butt up."

I nodded and felt the raises on the walls on the way up to the bathroom. I found Thelma adjacent to the mirror. In a black dress, she applied a gentle layer to her eyes and powdered her cheeks, all while pausing to straighten her hair.

"She keeps bugging me to bug you to hurry up."

"Oh teller shut up, would you?" Thelma asked.

"I will. Mom?"

"Yes?"

"I love you."

"Love you more, babe."

They left in a whirlwind, and I scanned the house for any stragglers or ghosts. A rush came over my bones. I locked the front door, shut the blinds, turned on the TV, slipped the *Girls Gone Wild* DVD in, played the first scene, and unfolded in joyful chemistry.

Nice-Housing

From the beginning of August to the end of it, the heat and humidity stuffed dust bunnies in our noggins and suffocated us in our tight, sun-cooked skin. A few times we had enough twennies left over at the end of the week to take fun trips to the waterfront, with Thelma always finding enough to cover our seats for savoury Chinese wonton or rent some bullshit like *Norbit* or *March of the Penguins*, everybody gonked at the TV bloated and snoring by the time they trap Pingu in that hellish aquarium. Too beat from the humidity to catch house crickets jumping out the corner of our eyes. Nobody ever cleaned the stink growing on the kitchen counters cuz the stink grew in the sponges, in the black mudroom garbage bags.

For summertime work, Thelma, JD, and Jaybird redid cottage roofs in great middle-of-nowheres. They once took me to one, JD's dirty white Ford trailing another guy's car down a pitch-black forest road with hundreds of slender men bending the trees back and forth until we stopped at a cabin with moth-singed lights. The door opened to a crowd of fellas standing around a tall bong and a coke-dust plate, then a round of bro hugs and everybody's red-faced shameful cuz there's a little boy at the back of the pack. I watched these goofs salivating over Thelma's double Ds, ready to rip her from JD's grip if she starts looking too lost. Later in the night when I got hold of Thelma's pay-as-you-go cell, I called Kris, who was well versed in these types from Sunshine City, idiot cokeheads who'll sling a girl's name between two slurs and spit on it. "The fuck is she thinking, Code?"

I spent the remaining summer afternoons on the mattress, crouched over Future Shop flyers and taking scissors to advertised LCD TVs, surround-sound packages, and Xbox 360 bundles (New *Halo* 3! Only $59.99), and gluing a mean collage, running upstairs when the red deals unrolled from elastic-wrapped newspaper sheets. Then Louise began packing up her room, along with her half of the rent.

The combination of Louise moving out and my SOS beacons from the pay-as-you-go led to the decision that Kris would take me in. She made the trip up in O Touro's Jimmy and she could see that Mindi was jittery, giving her whatever leftover furniture she had.

For the first few months of living in the house on Coldwater Road, I flopped on the futon in the living room and stayed up late praising my hush-hush *Hustler* pages and picking from cases of bootlegged horror shows and used DVDs, maybe playing the copy of *Twilight Princess* Julian got for GameCube. We took trips to music stores, where my brother could slide a band poster up his coat's arm, or to Sunshine City's waterfront, where my sister and

I took selfies on a point-and-shoot she bought when she won four hundred bones at a casino in Port Perry or something. We'd lean against a beach willow or a statue and Kris would offer me new knowledge gleamed from her magic mushroom trips, from the scriptures of Carlos Castaneda, about the DMT she dreamt of trying, maybe one day when we move down south, eh, Code? The rooms filled with her pals and their chatter. The halls always stunk like Lysol wipes, powerful perfumes, and the faint comfort of Hulk the bong. We got *Rock Band*, and Kris dedicated her Tuesdays off work to hosting parties that packed the place with screaming drunkos. Doritos rebranded. Lots of Domino's Brooklyn Style pizza to go. On the weekends we cleaned up, and Kris would open all the windows and blast her stereo. She'd play *Welcome to Jamrock* by Damian Marley, and our favourite song was "Road to Zion," cuz the melody stirred something in us and Damian reminded any half-bads out there to keep on walking. We had a coin laundry a few houses down and slipped envelopes of cash under its locked door for rent. This was nice-housing done right. This was the good life.

I returned to Monsignor Lee and Kris came to my seventh-grade parent-teacher meeting straight-faced, the teacher calling her brave and applauding us for packing a lunch every day. He told me not to worry about homework.

Kris made sure we went to school cuz she knew where it could lead us. But Julian dropped out and reasoned that selling dope and other nefarious things was the best he could do until he found an odd job that paid better. A nerve-curdling yellfight broke out between him and Kris, and she kicked him out that day. They both stayed pissed about it for months.

When Julian left to live in his friend's basement, I took his upstairs room. Little changed at first. I began to wash my hands a lot, dozens of times a day to the point they cracked with blood and chapped whenever I clenched my fists to brace myself for the walk home after the final school bell ding-donged. Anytime my hands felt clammy or unclean, I soaked them under cold water. Kris caught me doing this in the bathroom a few times and shut off the running faucet.

A few weeks before Christmas, Mindi showed up to Coldwater Road with layers of long johns under her coat and a hiking bag strapped on her back, just wanting to stay a few days at most. And only cuz JD took off to BC after all. She told me everything was going to be okay and I watched her face relax and contract with brain pics as she slept on the leather couch.

About a week in, I woke one morning to a big yellfight between Mindi and Kris. And what did I see when I came downstairs but Mindi with her backpack and snow pants on, trekking into the tundra of Coldwater Road, then turn a corner and bam. Gone.

I asked Kris why she did that. She took a hit from Hulk and began getting ready for work, telling me that some people never learn.

For my thirteenth birthday that year, Kris let me have two friends over, so I invited a pair of them from Monsignor Lee, exotic to me in their ordinariness. I was fascinated by the type of middle class they inhabited, the way they breathed in and out and wanted to grow up to be orthodontists and gym teachers and how they got flustered if you asked them too many personal questions in a row. I endlessly wondered what kind of home raises someone who wants to install metal in a mouth for a living.

They sang "Happy Birthday," and I blew out the candles and wished for us to keep living the good life on Coldwater Road. To keep nice-housing.

Not long after that, we were getting ready to go shopping one day when Mindi called Kris and told her she was taking me back. After being moved off a waiting list for some west-end housing, she needed Julian and me in tow to seal the deal. She showed up unannounced, booted down my sister's door, barged in, grabbed me by the arm, and took me outside. The thinness of her wrist bluffed her fierce grip. We had places to be but nowhere to go. Mindi looked like she'd just woken up from the deepest of sleeps, and her hair stood up and out and the heartbeat was blinding me to tears, and it was in that moment I knew there was more to come from this half-bad living.

Interlude

WHITE REGALIA

If anybody asks about white regalia, tell them to imagine the newfound confidence after the fridge lifts off a recent divorcee's back. Or what that divorcee slips into before they step out the door to face the hunger moon. Maybe it is the farmer's brain pic every time they meet the horizon and shove callused hands and a rusty shovel into the land with all the love they can muster so that their children live to hug the future. The puff after puff of smoke that outlines the ghosts within. How to embrace the sizzling belt. The happy dance of not giving up, after saying Fuck it, I want to know. The infinite singularities that make you you.

Tell them white regalia is an impossibly perfect silhouette. All that sexy shit at the back of the closet. Piquancy and schmaltz on a hot day. The pair that feels best. The waabishkaa ones the boogie monster steampresses on disco night. When the whip drifts nice and the ankle-to-cuff ratio is just right and the dash of bling never lifts off the collar. The brilliant panache and ease of a swinging hoop. All those hoops and cones jangling into April's showers. The duck and slide and pumpfake that a seasoned half-bad can pull off with ease when the buckle comes. Anything paid in advance is white regalia. It's what the kid dons to crush mission after mission on legendary mode. The mode itself.

Above all, tell them white regalia is a red herring. A total knock-off. Complete letdown. The brief yet annoying buzz of the season. Tough to buy but easy to sell. Yet another cautionary tale full of hasty generalizations. A decidedly public meltdown. Too heavy to handle but held just the same. The brick wall waterfall when someone thinks they've got it all. But they don't. They never will. Cuz they'll never get past the wagging finger. The paywall. The City of Law. The blind harrier. The dulled thumbprint of a sightseer on icy braille. The wrong turn. The snake eyes on loaded dice. The flash across the screen before the dead battery. The lightning behind an unmarked gravesite. The off-grid encounter. The middle one flanked by pinky and thumb. The locked chest. The maxed-out stats. The nastiest trap card. The rumble that hijacks the interior. The reset to factory settings.

If someone asks, tell them white regalia is the password to the spectacled troll's computer in *Jurassic Park*. The mob boss's clipped goodbye before the screen cuts. The bullet-brained homie in the dilapidated bathroom standing up. Another show cancelled after the first season. What they don't see when Master Chief takes the helmet off. Tell them whatever they want to hear. Probably made their mind up by now anyways.

PART IV

BABY MINOTAUR

Call It Camping

From shotgun I watched the main roads connect and fall away from one another as Mindi drove us downtown. Her signature perfume layered with the stink from our storage unit. "You're gonna love the house, babe. It's in a great neighbourhood."

"Which neighbourhood?"

"A new one . . . You'll see."

Deckhands, vagrants, and rovers bopped up and down the brick lanes of Main Street. The clouds gathered around Sunshine City and began to spit, filling it up with humidity.

Us two drove through the suburbs at ninety kilometres an hour, flying by hillside homes with the occasional garden flamingo, eventually pulling up to a WALKER VILLAGE sign and rows of townhouses. We turned onto the first row and passed bare-skinned villagers peering down at us from their concrete porch steps. At the last unit on the left, Mindi woo-hoo'd and announced that we'd made it. I hopped out and peered at the tricycles and scattered toys, making out the low whine of a screaming baby a few units down.

Within an hour, we'd moved our collective possessions into the living room with the help of a friend from Teletech, a call centre where Mindi worked. Milk crates full of old client files, camping chairs, pillows, mosquito coils, garbage bags of clothes. Box of photo albums. All that stuff in the Jeep. Mindi had stacked her nutrition books to the right of the living room entry, side by side. Deepak Chopra books on quantum healing. *Body Worlds: The Anatomical Exhibition of Real Human Bodies. Wheat Belly. Anatomy of the Spirit.*

I took off to the top floor to check out the bedrooms. Two rooms, one smaller and one larger, sandwiched mine. The big one would be Mindi's and the small one would be Julian's. I fingered the sticky bits and splotches on the walls. While Mindi went out to get beer and pizza, I masturbated, found "fuck u fag" carved inside the closet, pulled out some CDs, and began to place them in stacks along with some books against a wall. I jumped up and down a few times. Then I went downstairs, past the living room, whipped around the foyer, and into the basement. Nailheads stuck out the foundation.

Carcinogenic dust and the sweet, barely breathable sour must smacked some sneezes into me. The basement had a sliding glass back door that led out to our yard. I went up into the kitchen and found a fly dying, so I drowned him in soap and cut his wings off. I cleaned up the mess before Mindi showed up with a six-pack of Miller Genuine and a large box of pepperoni. We opened some more boxes and then the unit got hot, so we opened some windows. We took a break and sat on the kitchen floor cuz we had nowhere to sit.

"How much is it?" I asked.

"Eighty bucks a month. Finally, a place just for us!"

Mindi leaned against a window and sipped her beer, taking it all in. I read an issue of *Official Xbox*, gawking at games and to-buy lists for Christmas filled with pricey computers and partisan white-flag op-eds on the sixth-generation console wars, the curse of sequels, and how to assess bad endings. I read them closely over and over, spotted grammar issues, missing letters. Mindi lit a few tea lights and closed the windows. We inflated the blow-up mattress with our lungs and shared an unzipped sleeping bag like we did in Barrie. I fell asleep to her sorting files and creating piles and stacks. And then she shook me awake.

"Get up, Cody. Breakfast, babe. No better way to start the day!"

I couldn't run from the morning muck in the mouth and the rumbling of the stomach. I followed her into the kitchen and sat on the floor. On a stove coil was a bent coat hanger with a piece of Dimpflmeier sitting overtop. The hot tip of the brass hanger toasted the bread. Mindi flipped it to toast the other side. She knifed a square of butter and let it ooze from the heat.

"Learned this trick from my dad," Mindi said, smiling at the memory. She grabbed the bread off the counter, turned around, and paused mid-step. "Oh. Hold on."

She tossed the coat-hanger toast on the counter and went to the living room, picked up a milk crate, and dumped work files and folders onto the carpet. She did the same again with a second crate, and then she brought them over and flipped the crates upside down. She made seats.

"Here, babe. Eat."

We ate our coat-hanger bread. It was pretty tasty.

"Isn't this fun? It's like camping a little, isn't it? Let's call it camping. Ha."

Played the Pocket

Slowly us two settled into the unit. Mindi quit Teletech and got a job serving at Caddyshack's, made enough in tips to get me drum lessons in the upstairs of a music shop in downtown Sunshine City, where the drum teacher patiently watched me through a pair of Ted Bundy glasses.

I couldn't strike the kit without fumbling or losing focus. Could nail three tom-toms and then hit the hi-hat just fine, but would mess up on the big tom. I kept saying sorry, but the drum teacher just sighed and said "Try again." Again and again. Eventually he put his hand up to signal me to stop.

"Well, that's our time for today. I know it's only your second lesson, but you need to keep up with this pattern now, you hear me?"

I wanted to drum, and I wanted a drum kit. I wanted to drum in bands and parades. I wanted all of it. In fifth grade I'd watched Tré Cool, who I believed to be the best drummer alive, drum for a hundred and thirty thousand people in Milton Keynes—over and over again—on a live DVD, owning every fill and song and rocking every fan. In one particularly moving scene, he stared into the camera and said he was watching all the drummers out there. And all included drummers like me who didn't have a drum to beat. Back at Coldwater Road, I naturally went straight for the drums whenever we played *Rock Band* and could play most songs on Hard difficulty. When our show got too loud for the baby in the apartment underneath us, we had to lift the kit onto the coffee table. When us three would visit Sunshine City Public Library, I'd YouTube this Australian kid around my age banging out OK Go songs on a black seven-tom kit in a real studio until Kris came and said time to go, Code. But I didn't want to go. I wanted to jump through the screen and into that drum seat more than anything else.

After I told my drum teacher all this, he said that's great but repeated that I needed to practise on a kit at home if we would continue meeting.

"My mom and I just moved to a new place," I said. "The walls are thin."

"Use what you can then. Buy a pair of Vic Firths on your way out and set up some pillows on the floor around your feet. Anything. You need to bang on something to get the pattern."

On the way out, I broke a twenny Mindi gave me for lunch on a pair of 5A American Classic Vic Firth sticks. I hit the brick sidewalks of downtown Sunshine City as I headed toward Caddyshack's. I was at a set of lights when a sweaty rover with a nasty sunburn shook a coin cup at me.

"You-have-any-change-for-a-fella-to-get-some-food-and-shelter-tonight?" Salt-and-pepper beard and a bit of dirt on his forehead. I had ten bucks left. I handed it to him cuz I was still high off buying the Vic Firths. "Here. It's not much."

"God bless your soul. Door to good fortune will open for you soon." He took the ten and off he went running down Main Street.

I pushed open the Caddyshack's door and saw Mindi doing laps around the bar, grabbing pints and serving oldheads who'd been drinking on the stool tops all afternoon. Beyond the bar were bathrooms, a vintage golf arcade game, and a door to a busy patio.

Mindi spotted me shortly after she poured another beer into a pint glass. "Hey, babe! Give me a sec. Go sit at any open table. I'll be right here."

After Mindi took the regulars' orders, chatted up the new walk-ins, and asked her co-worker to cover for a sec, she came to give me a big hug. She leaned against an edge and drummed a coaster against the table. Her nails and face were painted and made up. She grinned. I grinned back.

"How was your lesson?"

"Good. He wants me to keep practising, so I bought a pair of drumsticks and gave the change to a homeless man."

"You did what?"

"I gave the change to a homeless man."

"Why?"

"I don't know. He looked like he needed it."

"Oh." She looked around Caddyshack's, then pushed herself off the table. "Never a good idea, babe. Don't ever do that. I just worked an hour for that money."

"Sorry."

"It's all right. Anyway, come out here. There's somebody I want you to meet."

Mindi took me out to a patio table and introduced me to Leacock and his roommate. "You can hang with them until I finish my shift, mmkay?"

"Nice to meet you, Cody." With a confident smile and grip, Leacock pulled a firm shake out of me.

"Your mother tells me you like drumming," said the roommate, who sipped his beer and scratched his soul patch, leaned on the patio glass.

"A little," I said. "Just learning right now."

"Well, we got a drum kit at our place. If you ever need one to practise, come by anytime."

"What's your kit?"

"Custom. I worked hard and saved up for it. Cost me a couple thousand. Who's your favourite drummer?"

"I like Tré Cool. Some drummers on YouTube."

"Well, I think you two are coming over tonight. So you can practise then."

I went back into Caddyshack's to wrestle with my math homework on a high top, borrowed a dollar from a server to play R.E.M.'s "Man on the Moon" on the jukebox, which was what Kris liked, and ate a club sandwich with a side of tongue-scalding fries. Eventually Mindi's shift ended and we went with Leacock and Soul Patch on a trip to the grocery store and the Beer Store. They came out from the latter with a two-four of Bud and a six-pack of Miller Genuine for Mindi.

Soul Patch drove and parked the car in front of a white-panelled two-storey. We walked inside to a living room with bouncy couches and a flatscreen that everything pointed toward. Records neatly tacked high onto the walls and a computer blared music from a repeating playlist on the other end of the room. Cigarette stink hung in the air. In one corner of the room was a steel teal-skinned drum kit. The custom.

A squawk came from the kitchen, where two bright feathered birdies argued in a corner cage, hanging above their dried white crap on flyers and old issues of the *Packet & Times.*

"Yes, the buggers," Soul Patch said. He let a bird out and onto his finger. "They make a lot of noise. It's fine though. Good party hosts."

He ripped open the cases and pulled out three beers and tossed one to Leacock, one to Mindi, and one to me. Just joking.

They cheersed, sipped, and then sipped again. The heartbeat sank under the horizon. More of their friends showed up and a fire started in the pit out back. Two more cases of Canadian arrived and emptied out: the first slowly, the second quickly. The birdies belted at the houseguests from their tiny kitchen cage, trying to get a piece in.

At some point, Mindi and Leacock got into position for a photo that she ended up using as her Facebook profile picture for quite some time. Mindi in front of Leacock, his arm wrapped over her neck and chest, the trust in him, the assessment that here was the one.

I went back into the house and found Soul Patch at the computer picking a tune and sipping a beer. He had no computer chair.

"Your drums are nice."

"Well, jump on and practise, brother."

After moving to the corner, I grooved into the cushioned seat. Classic records from the eighties and the nineties hung above me on the walls. In front of me were six to eight toms, a big bass drum, and multiple hi-hats. Wiry jazz brushes and chipped sticks poked from a bag. He even had a cowbell attached to it. I brought one of my new sticks down on it.

He turned off the music and asked me to show him what I got.

I played the test pattern. But it didn't sound good and before I could finish a second time, Soul Patch raised his hand, cuz that's what drummers do.

"Let me show you."

He took the sticks from me, took the seat, thumped the bass drum, and ripped the custom kit. I stood at the side of it.

"This is the pocket," he said. He smacked down on the bass drum and the hi-hat and puffed his cig. "Thump your bass drum every time you smack the hi-hat, and tap the snare after four hits." He played it slow for me. "Eventually, you can branch out and get crazy." His sticks ran up and down the kit and hit the toms like jazz and the cowbell bopped and he banged the crash. The drumming hit me with waves of vibrations and then he slowed down. "But you always have the pocket."

I nodded.

"Your turn."

I sat down and tried the pocket and nailed it. I picked up the speed.

"You got it. Keep practising. I'm heading back out there."

"Can I use your computer to look up some songs?"

"Yeah. Don't ask. Cheers, Cody."

After a couple hours, everybody took off except for Mindi and Leacock, who stumbled past me to sit on the living room couch.

"Play another one, babe!"

"Play nice and loud, bud!" Leacock said. "Give us that full concert experience."

I played the pocket. Mindi's eyes closed and her hands drummed some air sticks, but she was still hitting the test pattern. As I watched Mindi and Leacock hitting second base, I played the pocket. I stopped playing the pocket. They stayed on second.

In the morning, Soul Patch let me wake them up with the drums.

Between the Door and the Frame

Any buck who knew O Touro well enough could tell he was doing himself dirty again. Who could miss the extra cartilage that followed his every swallow, or the occasional twitch that surfaced on his limbs?

"Something the matter, son?" he asked from under a Leafs hat and tinted sunglasses. Typical outfit after a bunch of big dos.

We met in public. Hugged quick and then found somewhere to sit. Picked the bench facing Sunshine City's *Island Princess*: a sightseeing riverboat docked at the bottom of Main Street. Something cute to see before walking the sandy planks to the city's sunburnt and greasy twin beaches to nowhere in particular. And of course, *Princess* is just sitting in port on schedule, which *Princess* does until the next spring's offering of grade eight graduations or summer resort tour groups come craving spritzers and champagne and some picture-taking in the middle of Lake

Couchiching, and then the boat goes off again. It's a nice picture, too. Nothing beats the *Island Princess* breeze.

It was the first day of fall. Perfect day to cruise the blues with O Touro. That last humid yet freakish wind that leaves the trees wheezing. Still warm enough that O Touro wore basketball shorts or cargos, his hairy Jell-O legs sticking out.

"We have no money," I told him. "I wear the same few pairs of boxers over and over. Julian said it's not a big deal and something he has to do too sometimes, but neither of us got lunches."

"Fuck she doing with the FRO then?" Perhaps Little Miss Dominion's most overlooked welfare task force, the Family Responsibility Office sorted out the unpaid child support O Touro owed Mindi, main way they touched base. In the last few years, FRO'd grown from acronym to arbitrator to mini boss nobody but myself could beat, and spawned a type of thinking in some folks that made them believe and speak to me as though I had the scoop on things. But I knew better than to show him where FRO went, so I tricked him best I could.

"Well yeah we use it," I said. "But toward rent and all."

Rent and all. Bulletproof. O Touro didn't have any way of checking how much rent-and-all was, cuz we had Geared-to-Income: the fare-and-well defence Little Miss Dominion equips its backload of battered-and-gaunt folk to defend them against some of the most unimaginable entropies. Plus it was none of O Touro's business, as far as myself or any of our mutuals were concerned.

"Time she got a better job, bud. I'm just trying to survive myself, Cody, back living in Debbie's spare. Fucking Hydro's fucked me right, too, so if you could talk to her about possibly . . . my back . . . could help me . . . telling you."

Always asking me to cut the cuff. Try and Lysol-wipe his chiselled name from FRO's slate. But no harm to him cuz most half-bads tend to attract third parties anyways. Though he did his best to game me, and boy could O Touro game. Too many let-me-borrow-your-MSN-chat-real-quick-to-message-Mindi-type tricks for me to not know any better. Though by then I knew how he handled a pan and ran a rodeo, and so I said to hell slushing through any more of it.

Getting on was real easy back in Midland. New schools meant little-to-nil pressure to switch or iron the previous year's fits. Any kid could just walk right on into their classroom and tell everybody they went to the mall the day before. And who's to say otherwise cuz most malls carried a Winners. Plus public school kids didn't give two shits about that sort of crap. But my fellow eighth graders at Monsignor Lee Catholic were as curious as preteens could be. It amazed me how much fibbing and fake-newsing and what-do-they-mean-when-they-saying I had to do to explain where my internet connection was or why I reached into the navy bin so much. Why I never hit anybody back on MSN or got off Tutorial Island in *RuneScape*. I hadn't attended MLS since the fifth grade, so this meant they poked and prodded and tossed more questions my way than the agents who tried to take me from my big sibs. These fuckers picked up on my having crummy pencils and holes in my socks when we changed from indoor to outdoor shoes. At my old schools I could pilfer blueberry muffins and raisin bagels aplenty, but these kids eyeballed any hands that reached into the lunch bin for Bear Paws or a No Name peach cup.

"Bud?"

I flipped from the brain pic to see O Touro already behind the wheel of his Jimmy. There's nothing more O Touro than a Jimmy. Didn't matter what he filled it with either: tents and camping equipment, case of Bud or some No Frills, or even us three back when we got dropped off at his place on a weekend or for a couple days during winter breaks. It didn't matter if he brought us to some new girlfriend's kitschy trailer or a panelled basement or a summer unit below a cookie-cutter undergoing renovations, cuz most of his homes rarely bared any trace of him, mind a couple wallet pictures by his bed or framed in silver beside the TV. Always a TV with the Leafs losing badly on it.

"I better go," I said.

"D'you need a ride somewhere?"

"I'll walk."

"Please just let me help."

"You could drive me home, but we should get going."

He nodded. I hopped in shotgun.

The Jimmy hit all three sets of red lights on our way to Walker Village. The dips in the road sent us up and down, up and down. We didn't talk small or talk big. We didn't talk at all. And then O Touro pulled in, so I hugged him goodbye, rocked shotgun shut, and glided toward the shin-breaker concrete entrance of the townhouse, the last one on the left.

I pried the screen door open. They had Rock 95 on full blast. Heard some back-and-forth yelling underneath but couldn't say whose from the foyer. The higher-pitched pitter slipped into the ear like Mindi's, but was more floaty and freed, like singing. I kicked off my shoes and headed toward the Muskoka tunes and the voice or two I heard coming from the living room, even though a big part of me didn't want to go.

I took inventory: our kitchen patio table we found roadside glimmered and oozed all goosebumps goop with sticky, stinky amber booze. Around the table were two brooding dudes poofing a doob who couldn't quit giggling at jackshit, long after they roached their joint to a pinch. Between them was a Trouble board game they didn't finish, surrounded by empties they did. The die did not bounce. Trail mix, popcorn, and chips—shit I could have used to fend off those ghoulish school kids—spilt all over the fucking floor. Found wall stains and cracks in glasses that weren't there before. Someone flipped on the stove vents but clearly forgot to make anything cuz the sink had no dirties near it.

One brooding dude was a neechie named Snake who couldn't keep his eyes open. He just burped a bunch and then he bounced, and as he did I wondered why he had so many dirt stains on his jean jacket. The other dude was a curly-haired, bulbous jeweller who had a shop on Main Street. He sat up from his seat to leave, but before he did, he circled the kitchen and kept calling me a good kid. I could tell how buzzed he was cuz he held his head back with both hands. After he left, I went to check the main room, which is where I discovered Mindi making out with Leacock.

I was too shook to interrupt with anything other than some Qs with As I already knew: "Why you look like this when it's only four p.m.? What were those guys doing here? Thought you worked today?"

Mindi lifted her lips from the kiss, but kept her eyes shut tight.

"What?" She slurred and seemed unsure of her words. Leacock had some of her makeup on his shirt. She took a hard look at him, almost like she didn't recognize him.

I wondered if they'd recently poofed a doob. Or worse.

"Why you talking like that?" I asked. "Hello? HELLO."

She looked up at me again. Their mouths hung open in O's so low I just wanted to squeeze them. They looked a little looney-tuned.

"What are you even saying, baby?"

Saying floated out of Mindi's mouth and stayed suspended in the air, same way a heat mirage floats on a road. It freaked me out, so I froze up and stood there too long, then ran upstairs and shut the door. About a half-hour later, the two of them unplugged the Rock 95 and went up to her bedroom to blow out big, rattling snores.

I watched the most beautiful sunset collapse under crops of suburb roofs outside my window. I played a CD or two and decided to go back downstairs after I heard Julian and his duderonis coming through the front foyer.

"Want to play *Soul* with us, maybe order some pizza?"

"Hell yeah, I'm starving."

Julian worked in the city as a house painter and had the biggest paycheques in the house, thousand bones every time. But he blew through it, as was his wont to do at eighteen. Surf-shop clothes, an ounce or two of dope, new skate, and Xbox 360 games. He also ordered a shitload of Domino's. Julian asked if I was good with a Brooklyn Style, even though that's what we always ordered.

Deal was that I had to grab the pizza when the delivery dude came. The pizza bag hung between the door and the frame and

I tipped him as good as we could. Julian and his duderonis lit some candles in the living room and together we ate two or three greasy slices each. Made sure to wipe our fingers on our pants when it was our turn to play. I watched Julian and the homies take massively fat hits from the bong and then slowly float out the door over the course of the evening. Everybody began to leave and then Julian left for Sanyo and Leeroy's house out in Rama. I played *Soul* for a couple rounds, got sleepy, blew out the candles in the living room, and picked up Mindi's MP3 player from the table, spit-scrubbing the gunk off it. I found the Trews' album, *Den of Thieves*, grabbed a blanket from behind the couch, and laid down. I faded blinking out the cottage-cheese ceiling and listened and hummed along to the blue-collar hoser holler. And I would have passed out if it weren't for an inconsistent and rather loud pounding coming from above and shaking the cottage cheese.

I opened my eyes and paused the music. Somebody was drunk-cussing somebody else out real bad. Borderline yellfight. I got up from the couch and backed up to the wall. A couple GUSH-GUSH-GUSHes came smacking down the staircase, but she just stood there in the dark and stared me down, her hair standing up around her.

"Mom?"

She ambled down the stairs one step at a time, followed by Leacock shortly after. Leacock had no socks on his feet and no shirt under his zip-up. He mediated his insults through me.

"Some kinda mother you got here, Cody! Course she would cheat on me! Course she would."

"You better shut the fuck up, dude."

"Bro!" Leacock karate-chopped the air and curled his lips over his teeth. "She fucking cheated on me, Cody. She's been talking to that Native bastard, Snake."

"Fucking idiot," she said. "I didn't cheat on you. Snake slipped something in my drink."

They yelled at each other and let me role-play as a half-bad adjudicator for ten or so minutes: Leacock-is-a-prick-who's-gonna-get-what's-coming-to-him, but not before Mindi-is-a-stupid-cheating-witch. I momentarily pulled away from them to text Kris the address, filling her in on what had happened.

"Fuck it, I'm outta here," Leacock said. "Buncha idiots."

"Oh whatever," Mindi replied. "Go on back to Mommy's house."

Leacock took off in just his zip-up and runners, and then it was just us two.

"I'm moving out."

"No you're not."

My cellphone rang.

"Give me that."

I answered the call, but before I could say anything more than Kris's name, Mindi had yanked the phone from me. We war-tugged until she buckled, lost her grip, and let the phone slip from her fingers. But when I went to check the call, the entire screen had filled with cell light so bright I almost fell in.

Mindi moved toward me so I dodged her swing and I bolted up the stairs with that white light like a motherfucker. She was right behind me, and I could hear her lunging, could feel her digits brushing against my skin. I reached the bedroom door but couldn't lock it in time. She barged in and threw me into the hallway. Two of us slipped and I fell face first on the top step. My lips and cheeks scrambled and swelled. Somehow I managed to get up and away from Mindi's grip, but I wasn't thinking and jumped the flight of stairs. I landed on an ankle hard enough to drop the phone. Then I jumped from the landing and down the next flight, smoking a pinky toe off the heater in the foyer. Mindi came GUSH-GUSH-GUSHing behind me. I managed to turn the knob and was about to open the door when I was yanked by the neck and pried from the exit. And then it came.

I'll admit everything goes a bit blurry from here. There was the squealing and the crunchy heat after my ear caught between the door and the frame, followed by a rush of white burning inside me.

Mindi took me by the arm into the living room to calm me down as I struggled to breathe and blew saliva out in big heaves. The mouth goop was so thick I couldn't even tell her to go away.

A set of red lights burst through the curtainless living room windows. It was O Touro's Jimmy pulling into the wrong unit. I got up and banged on the window until Mindi yanked me away. A moment later, the front door opened and up the foyer stairs came Kris in a hoodie and sweats, trying to assess what had happened.

"Go on and get outta here!" Mindi said.

"You better shut the fuck up right now," Kris said. "Oh god. Your ear, Code. Let me check your ear."

She took me to the bathroom, balled up some toilet paper, and dabbed it under hot stinky tap water to wet the swollen part. Mindi stood in the doorway, the *saying* from earlier still wavy in front of her. In the bathroom light, I could see her eyes went yellowish and her tan was sickly. The buckle was done with her.

"You go on and get outta here!" Mindi told her off as best she could. "You're not fucking taking him anywhere! He's my son. MINE!"

"How can you seriously think that any of this is good for him?" Kris asked. "Look at him! Look at you!"

Mindi stepped further into the bathroom, in front of the toilet, but she didn't do anything.

It was a tiny bathroom, one Little Miss Dominion didn't make for more than one person to fit in. It began getting hot. Mindi opened her eyes. It was the eyes that stayed with me.

"You can't leave me alone!" she said. "Please. If you go, that's it."

"You're on some drugs, aren't you, Mom?"

"They slipped something in my drink!"

Kris handed me the wet wad of toilet paper and her keys and told me to wait in the Jimmy. I slipped on a pair of sandals and went down the concrete entrance toward O Touro's Jimmy and heard glass shattering and cutlery clattering against the kitchen floor. Or at least I think I did.

I had the door ajar when Mindi came out without any shoes on. Her face paled in the bug-swarmed and orange Walker Village lights. She hugged me over the shoulders, tighter this time, and began crying uncontrollably, looking as if she'd just woken up from a very bad dream.

"Goodbye, son. Thank you for everything," she said and then looked up and raised her folded hands to the sky. "And thank you.

I'm done now. It's my time." Before I could say anything back, she ran into the townhouse. And in the quiet of the row, I heard another familiar, unfriendly, and altogether unsettling clattering happening from inside. So I hopped in the Jimmy, locked the door, and waited.

Wrong Turns in O Touro's Jimmy

Kris whipped O Touro's Jimmy out of Walker Village so fast that I blinked and missed the whole row. Just up ahead was Leacock, steadily stumbling back to his mother's house. We passed him. Kris believes he was still in the unit when she left, but I remember only me and Mindi there. So pick whichever iteration is more appealing, I guess.

We took a turn down a suburb road and then another. We pulled into a random driveway, then pulled out of it. Did this a few more times. We were lost in a cul-de-sac. Worst of all, Kris didn't have her full licence.

"Should I try that way?" Kris asked me, pointing to Barrie Road.

I nodded. "Barrie Road leads to downtown. Let's take it."

We began talking about the apocalypse and what would come after.

"Doesn't matter anyways. They've set it out, Code. They're planning to remove large parts of the population within the next few years." I nodded and agreed. It was a novel virus, the fluoride, the Mayans, Zeitgeist, the illuminati, the corporate lobbyist liars. And when it all ended, it's not like they'd let a couple half-bads on the ship to Mars.

Eventually we hit downtown and pulled into Kris's Coldwater Road apartment. We put on a movie, and halfway through it, O Touro's newest girlfriend came in to check up on us.

"Your dad called the cops to Walker. He's with them right now. It's such a shame you kids are going through this."

We nodded but we both were annoyed.

When she left, I asked Kris, "What's her name?"

"I don't know. I have her number, though. I just put her name in as 'girl.'"

We laughed and started the movie back up, only to pass out before it finished.

A few days later O Touro picked me up and took me to Westview Place, and we drove to some woodlands with Debbie. In the middle of the woods, O Touro handed me his cell and told me who it was. I put the phone up to my ear. Mindi said she was at Lake Couchiching, feet hanging off the pier, and that she was ready to leave. That she loved me. That there was nothing left for her here anymore. That she was going into the water and not coming back out. And the whole time I stood there with her and listened. I did my best to understand, and then I understood. Kris had gotten a call too, had yelled at her. Then O Touro called the cops, and that's who found her.

Mindi spent a night in the hospital. Same padded room without a doorknob. Funny how he put them both in there.

I wasn't sure what had happened exactly. All I know is that I stayed at Kris's and walked to school from there for a few weeks until it was safe for me to go back to Walker Village. Once Mindi was home I went to the townhouse, grabbing the knob and wobbling the door back and forth between the frame and the foyer. I stepped inside.

"Mom?" I called out.

In pyjamas and with some hair frizzy like the electricity demo at the Science Centre, Mindi poked her head out from the corner and backed up against the wall.

"Hey, babe. How you doing?"

"Keeping up with homework and school." I spotted a pair of red Ed Hardy slip-ons with skulls in rows on the side.

"Good, babe. School is important . . ."

There was a box of shit in the living room. Magazines. Coins. Porno. Paul Auster novels.

"He's living here now, isn't he?"

"We're talking things over. He's out with his mother right now, but he'll be back soon . . ." She took a step forward. "I miss you, Cody. I want you back here. You have a room, plus your brother's still living here, too."

"I know you do, Mom. I miss you too."

Applied

That winter I did my best to live quietly in the townhouse. Leacock's constant and booming presence in the living room served as a deterrent to entering it. After the bus dropped us Walker Village kids home from school, I felt unwelcome entering our foyer and zipped by the main floor, heading straight upstairs to my bedroom until I was hungry enough to come back down after everybody went to bed.

I jittered and trudged through my final year at Monsignor Lee. My eighth-grade teacher insisted I apply myself so that I could enrol for academic rather than applied courses when I got to Patrick Fogarty, despite the fact that multiplication and the Pythagorean theorem troubled me deeply. After a night of kicking serious locust ass in *Gears of War*, I showed up to school in trembling, helpless fear of all eyes on me. I would have done my homework, but the buckle always came through to save me from the effort that persistent application requires, zoning me out with the little think. When

I got to class, with a pickling stomach digesting itself and the white and fuzzy tongue of dehydration curdling that last-second glass of milk, I entered the classroom with my head down. It wouldn't be long before the teacher, backdropped by the green chalkboard, was erasing yesterday afternoon's game of hangman and saying "Okay, guys, take out your math homework." Then all at once my fellow students would abandon me, whipping out a kaleidoscopic rainbow of binders and Hilroys flipped open to invaluable solutions and neat little numerical relationships, which might gather enough merit to land them a path to the good life.

But where I faltered in math, I had hope in reading proficiency. I could always read fast, and never struggled like some of my classmates or Muchachi's brother come reading time. And even though I wouldn't say it back then, I can partly thank Leacock for that. When I saw the Paul Auster novels in his move-in box, the cover of *Mr. Vertigo* worked some magic on me, enough to bring it up to Leacock one afternoon while Mindi prepped dinner. He said that he didn't like reading very much but loved reading Paul Auster books, especially *Mr. Vertigo*, said it was smooth the whole way through and that he'd be happy if I read it. So I did.

For days in the middle of that winter, when I came down with a mean case of the flu, I sat down with Walt the Wonder Boy and Master Yehudi, who taught him to levitate. Those two kept me company while I was bound to the mattress, even took me beyond it, around the universe and back. Walt was Harry Potter was Maniac Magee was Charlie Bucket. We all wanted to be Master Chief. In a sitting or two I read that book from cover to cover. Not all half-bads got this lucky.

Announcement

It was in the early days of spring when Mindi made her discovery. The heavy rain outside muddied up the dirt path that connected the townhouse rows together. I relaxed on the couch with my feet up on the coffee table. The carpet needed a serious vacuum and dishes filled the sink. Fruit flies and real estate flyers and the *Packet & Times* overtook the kitchen table.

I put on MTV's *The Real World: Brooklyn* and dreamt once again about living in a sunny penthouse in Red Hook, where the fridge and cupboards got stocked endlessly and housemates could follow wherever their ambitions took them. The buckle had just come for one of them, who'd just shattered the glass coffee table when Mindi came downstairs with a serious look on her face and said she had to tell me something.

"What?"

"I'm pregnant."

"You're pregnant? What do you mean you're pregnant? How?"

"I don't want to talk about it right now."

After that, Leacock came downstairs and into the kitchen. He opened a cupboard and filled a glass with tap water. I heard the suction of the freezer and out came a tube of ground beef he threw on the kitchen table. Then he went back upstairs to their bedroom and closed the door.

Meu Velho Homem

In the spring I spent a weekend with O Touro, and a pregnant Mindi dropped me off at the motel that doubled as cottages for Hydro One employees. O Touro had a new tattoo, which said "live to learn/learn to live" on either side of barbed wire that wrapped around a walrus-white bicep. He showed me his room with its single bed and a duffle bag of clothes and construction boots on the floor and the few silver-framed photos of us three on the dresser. It was peaceful. I hadn't seen O Touro since he was staying in Debbie's spare but felt comforted to see he kept close what mattered most.

Since his room was too small for us both, we slept on the couches in the living room, and at night he snored. I watched *Shrek* for the millionth time and ate as many bowls of Lucky Charms as I could in one sitting. The Hydro One dudes he didn't introduce me to ghosted around us and it was clear O Touro had asked to borrow their common room that weekend.

On the morning of the last day, we took a canoe out of the motel shed and walked down to the lake. We plopped it down into the water and hopped in without life jackets, paddling out to the middle. Our paddling stayed mostly consistent, steady, unnoticed in the breeze. O Touro's rowing drove the canoe and compensated for my shaking contributions. But no matter how much I struggled, he never complained or gave me shit. He just kept rowing and working out his shifted discs, just learning to live.

After ten minutes, we tossed our shirts at our feet and listened to the water birds clacking, telling us to keep going. We kept going.

Graduation

Despite the growing tensions at Walker Village, Kris would frequently swoop in to scoop us, taking me and Julian out to dinners, to the movies, to chill with her casino friends, to go on hikes along off-beaten trails. She even saved up enough to take us to our first-ever concert, the muddy and poncho-rocking Edgefest at Downsview Park. Us three were so antsy and thrilled to gear up in Cousin Leeroy's car for the day, and I couldn't stop lint-rolling my pants the whole time, so excited to hear the songs we knew by heart. Kris knew how to smoothly butt in lines so Alexisonfire could autograph a heartskull T-shirt. She took photos whenever a blow-up doll or greasy kid surfed the crowd or when Leeroy gave me secret bunny ears. Seeing those photos, I noticed that I'd finally grown into Julian's favourite neon-green hoodie and that since the dentist shrunk the gap between his teeth he was learning to smile all over again. For a long time, he never smiled for photos.

After Edgefest, Kris took me to the mall in Barrie to pick out my graduation outfit. Naturally, we went to Le Château, where I procured a lime-green linen button-down, a discounted black fedora, and black suspenders. I completed the outfit with a Spitfire belt I borrowed from Julian for the night and black skinny jeans purchased from the girls' section at Stitches in the Sunshine City Square Mall. Maybe it was the smell or crispness, but new clothes felt like candy to me.

I ironed my outfit, straightened my hair over one eye like Pete Wentz from Fall Out Boy, sprayed myself with a stinky canister, brushed my teeth, and got ready to step out for the big night. Mindi called out to me from the couch in the living room, backlit by the sun coming through the windows. She flipped through the channels and asked me what time we should head over for the graduation.

"My dad's driving me. Remember?"

She looked out the window with her hands in her lap, assessing the view, and told me to have a nice night. It was then I knew that this issue of selection would always come up before future life events and graduations, weddings, court orders, whatever. I'd have to pick between them, knowing that no matter who I picked, one would feel overlooked.

The graduation began at the school but then O Touro drove me over to the *Island Princess* loading site. Kris took photos of me in my Le Château garb, sandwiched between my classmates in their oversized suits and chiffon dresses. O Touro looked on from the crowd of adults, the evening rays beaming off his shades. The littlest grin.

Together against the Storm

In the summer my graduating class at Monsignor Lee got bused out to orientation day at Patrick Fogarty. I watched my fellow classmates disperse among the busloads of kids from other grade schools, congregating, synthesizing, and beyblading to their respective circles and melting away into the rest of their lives. For most, the panorama of grade school friendships were not expected to outlast those oh-so-fateful summer months into the first semester of 2009, let alone the four years that followed.

In September I showed up to my first class, ready for the rest of my life in a blue Winners flannel, the top of my hair unsalvageably split-ended yet straightened to infinity and beyond, toting Julian's old and doodled-on binder. By the end of the first week, I found my own circle of half-bads: petite scenesters who'd outgrown their Old Barrie Road and South Ward townhouses, fearless troubadours man-of-the-housing for their no-show O Touros out in the half-bushes of Washago, isolated gamers safe in their caves,

Filipino footworkers, and half-baked visionaries from the Mount Slaven and West Ridge suburbs. Together, the half-bads split from the morass of boredom and home life to assemble, whether at somebody's house or at the grease beach hill downtown or way across Sunshine City to battle-rap in their freshest, crack wack jokes, walk back and forth along the boardwalk or through downtown, point out a pair of fake Sky Highs, catch a fight that got too scary after a few blows, film another even goofier one behind the Little Caesars, and party hard in the bush.

Attending Patrick Fogarty was doubly sweet cuz I didn't have to pack a lunch or worry about buying back-to-school clothes, mind on civvies days. But within the first few weeks, I struggled to blend into high school parties without any doob poofing or beer drinking, a conviction I'd set for myself after a few weeks of Hulk's company and the way *saying* floated overhead. Crushes and buddies invited me to parties and then sharply pivoted away when I didn't play flip cup, king's cup, or smoke dope. So I mostly kept my head down and got a job washing dishes at Brewery Bay, a joint downtown that served "Good Grub and Great Pub." Still does.

Among the few half-bads that my transition to straight-edge neurosis had granted me loyalty to was Pretty, a tall one who dug the same Southern Ontario hardcore bands as much as I did, whom some loudmouth bros nicknamed Skeletor cuz of his lanky strut. By the later years of Patrick Fogarty, we had formed Southpaw with a few other left-handed pals. We gathered in the addition built off Pretty's stepfather's garage and played our instruments badly while I shredded and fried my voice screaming the lyrics I wrote about a non-place I named "the badlands." Despite all signs to the contrary, I saw Southpaw as my one-way ticket out of Sunshine City, an antidote to the staleness that Pretty and I saw examples of everywhere: Slouching Worker Eats Fry from McDonald's Bag Alone in Truck. Teenage Parents in DC Skate Shoes Push Stroller through Downtown Sunshine City Swearing at Each Other. Local Senile Sits in Food Court Every Day Wearing Same Grey Suit. This staleness was a feeling I'd known back in Happyland that was now coming into sharper relief: the elasticity of childhood possibility capsized by the hard crush of life, which began to feel more and more out of one's control.

Just as I was starting at Patrick Fogarty, Julian lost his job painting houses in Toronto, got a job barbacking at Tux II nightclub, and then lost that one too. To keep himself busy, he speed-ran through old-school Sega Genesis games, painted the white walls of his bedroom at Walker Village a brackish blue and mine a cloudy grey, did the best he could with the leftover paint and brushes. Even though he didn't have to, he let me have the bigger one, so his duderonis had to squish their way into his tiny square bedroom to get bloodshot and shoot for blood in *Gears of War 2* or win tournaments in *Skate 2*. Locust guts squirted all over the screen and many a three-flips got landed, Alexisonfire roaring from the stereo over burps and giggles and quips dripping with personalized insult, Julian's bedside lamp lighting the brackish blue with a soft yellow and wiggling the atmosphere like Jell-O. Bong puffs clouded up and mingled with the greasy steam of Brooklyn pepperoni from Domino's.

And then Julian stopped having his duderonis over and spent days on end lounging in the pyjama set that O Touro got him that winter, burning through classics like *The Godfather* or cycling through his favourite games and CDs. He often seemed distant and gauzy, his fingertips filtering brown crumbs of dank from an extra-big Ziploc bag, sitting there chilling a bit too hard.

"What's that?" I asked.

"Shake."

"You can't buy anymore?"

He shook his head and packed the rest of the shake and mixed it with tobacco from a Rama smokeshop carton until he had enough to take a hit. He took the hit.

One day that fall, O Touro picked us three up and took us to Hawk Ridge, which is where one lived if they descended from a Smith or a McCartney, hit the jackpot in slots, or helped turn a company into a country. O Touro asked us to dress nicely, so we did. I wore a peacoat from Winners and icy skinny jeans from West 49. Straightened my bangs over one eye and the mop up toward the heartbeat in the sky.

At Hawk Ridge, the Ontario Provincial Cops held a ceremony in the country club to award O Touro with a commissioner's citation for bravery, formally acknowledging that he'd saved a passenger from a burning vehicle on the highway after a tractor-trailer unit struck the car. Back in September, the car on Highway 401 had slowed down due to a lane closure and got struck from behind by the unit. O Touro saw the crash from his truck and pulled over, smashed the passenger window with a fire extinguisher, shoved his callused hands into the scorching metal, removed the seat belt, and saved her life. The driver didn't make it.

He looked so handsome that day in his suit, and what gets me the most is that he just wanted us three to be there with him. He wanted us to see that he could do the right thing.

That winter, when the used Xbox 360 O Touro bought me got the red ring of death, Julian and I devised a plan. When Mindi went to work that day, we'd get her to drop us off at Coldwater Road to grab the PlayStation 2 and our favourite game, *Champions of Norrath*, which we'd fallen in love with back at Auntie Meesh's McMansion cuz we could play at the same time, on the same team, and could both level up and get armour and spells and weapons for our characters as we slayed endless waves of baddies across Norrath together, backdropped by an epic soundtrack. Julian promised that our mission would bring us "hordes and hordes of fun."

Once we got to Coldwater Road, it was hard not to think about how good us three had it there. The endless water-based pancakes Julian made from the industrial bag of mix that came with the food-and-toy drive Kris's landlords threw for us. Us three cleaning together with the windows open and marathoning *Prison Break*. Hearing the constant buzz of Kris's cellphone to let work pals in for pre-drinks before they took off for Tux II, or hearing Julian usher in an entourage of skateboarding duderonis for vodka shots and a bong cough before they hit up Main Street buildings that needed spray paint. I always wished they'd take me with them, especially after Julian pointed out his tag on the way to the beach skate park, a ghostly SILENT in wispy white letters, same handle picked for his game accounts. The sound of his mind considering the uncertainties before him, dipping his toes into the ether of rumour and myth.

By the time we left the apartment, a blizzard had begun. Uncompromising and immediate, the shivers pouring in through our thin coats. Without gloves or hats or proper boots, we walked backwards together against the storm, Julian and me laughing through the flakes, him reassuring me about the hordes and hordes of fun that awaited us on the other side of the hill.

Provincial Report Card

Cody is able to read, making connections to help his understanding of the text.

Cody makes connections between *To Kill a Mockingbird* and the ones read on the Holocaust.

Cody has little understanding of the discovery of Canada and knowledge of who the leading European explorers were and their significance to the development of New France.

Cody struggles with applying this knowledge when speaking, writing, and reading.

Cody writes effectively, incorporating the techniques taught, showing an understanding of the importance of an entertaining beginning, building suspense, and satisfying story endings, using literary devices to help better visualize the story.

Cody is beginning to organize his ideas and develop his paragraphs.

Cody writes with some clarity.

Cody is encouraged to use the Pythagorean relationship.

Cody struggles to identify patterns and needs assistance to develop algebraic equations to solve problems.

Cody identifies angles and understands the relationship of angles within a triangle, however he struggles to solves problems involving lines, angles, and triangles.

Cody helped create a tableau presentation of "The Stations of the Cross."

Cody understands the importance of a frozen frame to carry out his story and confidently holds his position throughout the freeze frame.

Cody works hard in class, but struggles to get assignments in.

Cody understands that various individuals and groups have different opinions on environmental issues and the push-and-pull factors that affect where people decide to live.

Cody needs to better prepare for tests.

It is imperative that Cody complete all his homework so he can seek assistance in the areas most needed.

At times Cody needs to be reminded to use his class time wisely as he is easily distracted.

Cody created two- and three-dimensional works of art using pastels, washes, and magazines to create a mosaic.

Cody produced some nice pieces of work.

Cody is able to identify the benefits and risks that come with technologies and progress, and he is able to assess how they might affect various ecosystems.

Cody is respectful and mature.

Cody demonstrated some understanding of the events of Jesus's life and how to apply them to the role of discipleship within the Church.

Cody needs to approach new learning with a positive attitude.

Cody is encouraged to ensure assigned work is submitted on time for evaluation.

Cody showed a keen interest in political issues, particularly conflict diamonds and the war on terror.

At times, his late assignments affected his academic progress.

In the future, Cody is encouraged to complete all required assignments by their due date in order to attain better results.

Cody showed a particular interest in and ability for poetry.

Cody's ISU was very creatively done (90%).

Continue to use the planning sheets for your essays.

Cody's exam mark was 52%.

Cody works very hard in class and does well academically.

Cody has demonstrated some knowledges of how to apply Catholic Social Teaching when analyzing our role as stewards in the world today.

Cody is encouraged to improve his organizational skills.

Best of luck next year.

Miakoda

Kris hadn't spoken to Mindi much since the night she drove to the unit in O Touro's Jimmy. Thoughts of Mindi having another child with another man infuriated her. And then after I told her the baby was a fellow sister, she opened up about these dreams she'd been having of a baby girl with dark hair and light eyes. It was the same baby she dreamt of the year before, one who told her she'd waited lifetimes to join this one, a baby Kris at first thought was her own. The return of those dreams compelled her to message Mindi and come back into her life. On their makeup call, Kris explained why she was so upset, how that upset stretched from anger to fear. Anger about Mindi taking off from the Eastside of Happyland to live with Chiclets in Cobblestone Cottage, leaving Julian and me in her teenaged care. Fear that the baby would pull Mindi farther away from us than she already was. But she also told her she didn't want to live with anger and fear anymore. Cuz who does?

After their call, they met up for lunch and went shopping for the baby. Mindi told Kris she could pick the middle name, and after weeks of research and a sizeable longlist, she chose Miakoda, which internet baby name enthusiasts associate with the power of the moon. Kris even invited Leacock and Mindi over for a cozy photo shoot.

We had a baby shower with Leacock's family around Christmastime. I wore another flannel and a Banana Republic zip-up over it. Miakoda's due date was a week away, New Year's Eve. When we arrived, we took our boots and shoes off and walked into the kitchen, where everyone congratulated and hugged Mindi and Leacock, shook my hand, Kris's, and Julian's.

The kitchen was beautiful. The island countertop had stacked food trays and sleek pots they kept warm on heat-safe mats. The stove was one of those stoves with no coils on it. And the oven was inside the wall. Leacock's little nieces ran around, thrilled to put their ears up to Mindi's belly to listen for the kick while she sipped her ginger ale. Like always Kris documented the event, photographing Mindi smiling big and holding up pink little baby slippers. Julian and I sat at the kitchen bar overlooking the living room and watched Mindi open presents.

"It's weird that Mom's having a baby, isn't it?"

He shrugged. "Not really."

A few days later, I came home from chilling at Pretty's place and found Mindi in tears. I asked her what was wrong, but she just kept crying, and I could tell it was more than the hormones. I hugged her and waited but she didn't stop to say why, so I ran to Julian's room.

"What's she crying about?"

"He left," Julian said. "Went back home this morning."

"Why aren't you down there with her then?"

"Already was."

But it wasn't long before I heard Leacock's stomping feet around the townhouse again. And right on schedule, Mindi went into labour, just after the last and largest of the four minor lunar eclipses that year brought a giant marble blue moon into Terra's umbra. It was then Miakoda came down and out into the world.

Eavesdropping

One night in January, I was sneaking to the bathroom for a late pee when I heard Mindi's bedroom door smack against the closet, and there was Leacock standing in the hallway, arms stretched out toward me in sermon.

"You for real, Cody?" Leacock asked. "I'm up at five every morning so I can pay for this place. What are you doing? Waking us up at what time again? We got a baby in here, dude."

I had to make sure I'd never wake Leacock up or piss him off ever again, and so for the next few weeks, every time I had to piss at night, I went in one of the empty and crumpling plastic President's Choice water bottles we drank out of. Mindi found them one day while I was at school and threw them out. Lost it on me.

Another time, while Mindi and Leacock were out, I didn't take my shoes off cuz I forgot something before heading to Pretty's place for band practice. From upstairs I could hear Leacock and Mindi getting in, Leacock taking out another frozen tube of ground beef.

"Cody's got no respect, eh? Wonder who he gets it from."

"Oh come on," Mindi said. "He's just a teenager, that's all."

"No really. I mean, seriously. He doesn't get it, does he? What does he do? He steals my Ed Hardys and ruins them at camp, eats my fucking food. How'd he get a job washing dishes? Real fucking mint."

As Leacock continued to give Mindi crap and got ready to head to the backyard gazebo for a doob to poof and a cold one after a long day, I stormed down the flight and out the door.

Julian had moved out a few months before. He and Leacock weren't getting along, and their yellfights got so bad I just knew the buckle would come for one of them. And when it did, Julian went to go stay and party with Kris at Coldwater Road.

By then, Kris's co-worker Laura had moved into Julian's old attic room and convinced him to help paint it, even though they bickered the entire time. Then one day Kris had a guy stay over who she didn't want sleeping in her room, so she told Julian to go sleep up in Laura's room for a night. And that night turned into many.

Julian moved back into the Coldwater Road apartment, and Kris got him a job barbacking at the casino. Their rent shrunk when they split it by three, so they each could save a little and spend more. Shortly after, Kris got a nice raise and Julian got a promotion, and soon enough the much bigger apartment next door became available. The three of them moved in, only for Kris to move out and into her new boyfriend's place in Barrie a year later.

I felt left behind at the townhouse and wished I could somehow move in with Julian and Laura. Worse, I worried Leacock was right. Cuz that whole eavesdrop brought me back to all the times

I got desperate enough to steal or take something, like my sister's skinny jeans, or the loonies and toonies from Laura's giant crayon-shaped piggy bank, or the PlayStation 2 games from the kid on Christian Island, or Julian's collection of Xbox games to sell for the 360, or the *Majora's Mask* cartridge from Vandy. Or desperate enough to lie, like all the times I told my teachers that my grandfather died to get out of homework, never mind that I didn't even know what Velhote looked like. All those little thinks beginning to add up.

Baby Minotaur

Before I was born, O Touro got a tattoo on his shoulder of an eagle and a snake fighting for their lives. Underneath the fight were our three names.

Shortly after I turned sixteen, I googled "child abandonment" and in the second strip of images, I saw it. A baby minotaur.

"On your stomach?"

I nodded to the zapper, who traced a sketch on a waxed paper.

I'd saved up every buck I could. I convinced Mindi by convincing Kris, and accordingly prepared a ten-minute slideshow on Microsoft PowerPoint, complete with a long note to Mindi on Facebook. In June, she came in with me to the shop and signed off on the zap, under the condition that it was small. The appointment was booked for August with a few follow-up sessions in the fall. Only once did I ever flush with shock that some throwaway DeviantArt concept designed with a Wikipedia cocktail party knowledge of the minotaur allegory took up serious real estate on my body. But I went ahead with it, and it's still my favourite one.

Everybody in high school lost their virginity cuz of their truck. That baby minotaur was my truck.

Welcome to the Thunder Dome

In the spring before eleventh grade, the onset of the buckle was imminent, hovering in my periphery. I was steering clear of Leacock and the townhouse, which meant plenty of extra hours scrubbing dishes at Brewery Bay. After a doozy shift, I tapped on the chit board to get the attention of the closing cook.

"You can use the mop now," I told him. "I'm signing out."

"Sure thing, Scrody!" The cook scrubbed spotted sauce and grease off the heat lamp board with a steel wool pad. "Club wrap for your 99, right? Don't want those tomatoes still?"

I nodded. The trick for ordering a 99 was to ask before close. Even though they were cooks, many of them seemed to hate making food. Get a fuck-off from the grumpy ones for a 99 request during post-rush closed-kitchen cleanup. When I first walked in three years ago, the kitchen manager had made a big show of scaring me in front of the cooks by slamming his knife into the cutting block, catching the terror in my eyes when I flinched, and screaming "WELCOME TO THE THUNDER DOME, BITCH."

After I grabbed the club wrap and fist-bumped the closing cook good night, I slammed the dish pit's door and let wind lift the sweat away. The walk home from Brewery Bay was long, but after three years of closing, I could make it to the townhouse and eat the club wrap within twenty minutes. Twenty minutes to Xbox Live, the smuttiest clips and categories on Pornhub, and whatever else could wash away the dish grime. I ate the first half of the wrap by Mississaga Street and finished the soggy salty fries before I hit Westmount Hill. I pissed on the United Church wall and cut through the holy parking lot, eating the second half of the wrap after I hit Grenville and Marlisa Drive. Rows of trimmed lawns and soccer-mom minivans snaked up the suburbs, and my shadow came and went under streetlights. Beyond Marlisa was Barrie Road, and a right on Barrie Road took me to Walker Village, where I could hear villagers howling all night until a townhouse porch door slammed to let the buzzing lights and crickets hum me home. Six steps down a dirt path and into the townhouse row.

Somebody left the lights on. The gazebo net was wide open, unzipped. Again. I took a peek inside. Couple bottles of Miller Genuine on patio table. Mosquito coil still going.

I came to the front porch, pulled back the screen door, slipped off my Vans, and stepped into the foyer, passing another Miller Genuine or two on the kitchen table.

In her nightgown, Mindi was snoring peacefully on the couch. One of her nipples was out, which embarrassed me, even though it was just Mindi. My little sister slept in the tuck of Mindi's right arm like a football. A rush of pain came over my foot and I kicked the wood blocks underneath my damp socks down into the foyer. I turned around to head upstairs, ready to play some Xbox Live with whoever was still online. The homestretch to my room was only a few steps away, but I had to keep quiet or else I'd wake Leacock up, and I wasn't about to start pissing in any more water bottles. As I crept through the hallway, his snores grew louder. Something was wrong. I stepped into a warm wet spot on the carpet in front of my room and bent down to inspect it. Stunk like booze but was too red. I walked past the red marks on the wall and flipped on the lamp in my bedroom. Shoe prints dusted up the futon Mindi bought me for my birthday that year. The cushions had ragged cuts in the leather. I dropped my backpack beside my futon and slid my finger over the Xbox 360 power button and the sensor picked up my body heat. And then I swore I could feel the buckle coming.

My fingers poked through and appreciated a fist-sized hole in my wall. I smeared bits of debris over the back of the stand. I turned on the television, which Julian had bought me last Christmas. A rainbow of wiry colours dyed the room a crooked digital blue, a hue that couldn't show me what the Xbox 360 input demanded from the LCD pixels. Cracks in the Toshiba glass crisscrossed into a web. Blue, red, purple, and white lines wriggled and intersected at the pressure of a fist brought down on it. Leacock's fist.

Mindi waddled into my room.

"What did he do to my TV?"

"What?"

"Mom. My TV. Look at my TV."

"What are you even saying?" she asked. This time I knew she really meant it.

"Look at my fucking TV. How could you let him in here?"

Finally, Mindi saw the screen. Her face tilted and brought her index finger to her lips.

"Cody, you need to stay quiet, please—"

"Fuck you screaming about now?" From behind her stomped the man of the townhouse. Leacock was brighter than the bright red of those tomatoes I get the cooks to hold for my club wraps.

Watching them together, swaying between the door and the frame, the Miller Genuine stink emerged. And then it came.

"What did you to do to my room? This is MY room. MY futon. MY TV. The one place you're not allowed to go."

"You don't tell me where I can and can't go in my house, buddy. I pay the fucking bills here. You sleep on my queen mattress. Remember that. I work all day to keep this roof over your head! Heads!"

"Whatever, I'm out," Mindi said. She threw her arms up and went down the hallway toward the stairs.

"You that fucking drunk? I'm talking about my TV. The one you broke."

"Fuck you even saying, bro?" Leacock curled his little Miss Frizzles over his mouth and raised his right hand into a flat line, karate-chopping the air.

"Fuck you."

"Whatever, bud. Talk about it in morning." Leacock turned around and went after Mindi.

I opened my broken laptop and Skyped Pretty, who I knew would be up this late on a weekday.

"Dude, come play *Battlefield*," Pretty said. "We got a wild game going on."

"Would. But look what happened." I flipped the Gateway around and showed Pretty the TV and turned it back on.

"What the fuck is that? Grab your shit and come here. Now."

I closed Skype and looked around. I was frightened.

Three years ago, Mindi said I'd finally get my own room in the new house, and even though I had nothing to put in it, I grabbed an old CD stereo and a tiny kitchen television and that pair of Vic Firths and washed the swear words off the walls and thanked Mindi every day for this room. But it was Leacock's room that I'd walked into, and I should have known that before I ever got any funny ideas. That's the way things go in Sunshine City.

So I stuffed a backpack with clothes, slipped my Vans back on, and slammed the front door of the unit for the last time. I followed the dirt path and went up the hill. I ran beyond Mindi and beyond Leacock reclining in their backyard gazebo chairs, babbling through the open mosquito tent about something, resuming those two opened Miller Genuines. Their babble echoed out and faded away until it was nothing but the sound of my Vans hitting the ground of Barrie Road, running.

PART V

US THREE

New Day

I made it to Pretty's house just after two in the morning. He set me up in the music room, and instead of trying to get some sleep, I began tweeting threats and posting bitter status updates about the failed project that was the unit. I felt good about it until Julian called me and demanded I delete the messages at once. Otherwise a baddie could see them and incriminate Leacock and Mindi, let the agents take Miakoda away. Julian had intervened on many of my digital meltdowns during puberty, sometimes yelling at me about the danger of calling a half-bad a baddie and the real-world effects of getting in fights online with people I didn't know and people we did. Julian's voice was hoarse after a barbacking shift at Casino Rama, but he still conveyed the severity of my posting and the risk it posed to our baby sister's well-being and future. I stayed quiet as he raspily rhapsodized that keeping them up meant getting them in deeper shit than I wanted. So I deleted them and called Kris, who was now very pregnant and living at her boyfriend's place in Barrie, who in turn called the cops on Leacock. I woke up around noon, in a terrible mood, wondering what I was going to do.

Julian went to the townhouse immediately after his shift finished and told me it was a shitshow. In response to Leacock's fist-drop on the flatscreen, Mindi had lost it and smashed his—the one downstairs that they watched documentaries on after work—clean off the wall. Told him that if he gets to break mine, she gets to break his.

Knowing about the second busted flatscreen made me feel worse, thinking about how Miakoda would see the buckle coming so early. Julian said she was just playing with her toys in the destroyed living room, blowing bubbles and being a baby. Still wound up from his swing shift, he hoarse-screamed at Mindi and Leacock to clean up the mess before the cops came. The cops showed up anyway and made Leacock take anger management classes.

I moved into Julian and Laura's place in downtown Sunshine City. Massive open-concept with sixteen-foot ceilings. On the main street, too. Beside a pizza shop. Julian had ripped out all the carpet and installed warm laminate flooring, and by then he'd bought enough of his own furniture to fill up the entire space, including a cool faux-leather furniture set and huge flatscreen. I got promoted to host at Brewery Bay, bleached my hair and then buzzed it, much to Kris's chagrin.

Through the summer I dodged Mindi's calls and Facebook messages. Not that I didn't want to see her. I did. But I'd developed a stubborn habit of ghosting people rather than dealing with my shit, which I guess is the baddie way. Whenever O Touro called, we never talked about the buckle. Even when he hollered at me for jacking up the data charges on my Motorola Razr by trying to download All Time Low ringtones and torturing the 2-bit browser with searches for porno and the music video for Panic! at the Disco's "That Green Gentleman." I always hoped he'd bring the buckle up so that I'd know if I was crazy or not, if he saw it too.

When it came to Leacock, I had no plan to let him apologize. Toss him onto baddie island, get on the ferry, and go. I went back to the townhouse to pick up clothes from my room and saw him and some buddies upgrading the gazebo in the backyard, making garden boxes, and even though I tried to steer clear of them by using the front door, Leacock saw me leaving and asked how I was. Maybe it was the anger management classes or instructions from Mindi, but something about the way he asked, the wobble and uncertainty of his voice, made it clear he wanted to try again.

In August I finally gave in and let Mindi take me uniform shopping at McCarthy's in Barrie, where the parents of Patrick Fogarty students could shell out half a grand just to get their kids dressed for class, never mind the year's worth of lunches and extracurriculars. In my first year I benefited greatly from Julian's hand-me-downs. A shop called Sinergy had opened up next to the food court in Sunshine City Square Mall, but after a few semesters the school outlawed the knock-offs with their bootleg embroidery, a ban that unfairly affected us half-bads who'd gotten resourceful with our making-do, not to mention with forbidden tailoring and hemlines. This year the idea was to walk out of McCarthy's with at least three new items to blend in with the old rotation.

Mindi pulled into the driveway in Leacock's bullet-grey work van, and I hopped in and buckled up. Mindi had her hair done up and she was in comfy pants and one of her go-to shirts. She stayed quiet, telling me about my little sister's most recent developments, about the administrative tasks she was taking on for Leacock's business, about quitting smoking. About anything, really.

She adjusted the air-con, asking if the van was too cold, and in my periphery I could see she was still buckled up, hands on the wheel. Bracing for it.

When I didn't answer, she let go of the wheel and said my name. It was exactly then that she said she was sorry, fully and solemn. I didn't feel like hearing it at the time, so the *sorry* floated in the air. It travelled backward and forward in time. And when I finally looked over at her, I saw her looking back, hair bundled up in a scrunchie, her sweet hazels looking for mine. Sitting with her then, I knew just how lucky I was to have Mindimooye in this life, and even though I knew it wasn't my place to redeem her, I also knew I never wanted her to feel that way again.

Road to Zion

Kris slowed, signalled, and pulled onto Willow Crescent, and then just like that we were back in Happyland.

I scanned beyond the dashboard to see what had changed since O Touro packed that U-Haul, locked it up, and told me it was time to go on to the next one. As the house came into view, I could see it was split in two by some kid's basketball net at the edge of a newly gravelled driveway with an SUV smack dab in the middle. Kris kept pinching her gladiator sandal thong and slowed down after seeing the blue of a hundred moonlit oceans creep through the glass.

She gasped. "They actually painted it blue."

Whoever bought the place went for the bluest blue they could find. It was deep enough to drown out the honey nut stain. Bumps crawled up both forearms and into my shorts and through the damp uniform I wore to class that day.

We pulled into the cul-de-sac at the maw, the backyard in front of the car.

"Ten years, and still nobody is going to finish this thing? Didn't see the treehouse on the way in either, did you?"

"I guess they tore it down after we left."

The cedar fence he cut and began building had abruptly transitioned into single uneven posts and ended long before the backyard met the forest. O Touro always told us he would finish it one day.

I looked to the other end of the backyard, where our heartbeat-bleached swing set used to sit and rust, neglected by us three. A flame pit had replaced it.

I stepped out. Kris unfastened her seatbelt and stretched with her camera in her hand. She closed the driver door and loosened the strap off her shoulder a little bit. Baby Zion, in that considerable bump of his, the only bit of excess on Kris, expanded in the shadow he and his mom shared. One last hike before he joined us.

Out the four-door, backs to the blue house, we came to the end of Willow Crescent. It was evening, and we could hear only the crumbling gravel under our shoes.

"So. We going in or what?"

I nodded, and the cry of the Acura locking pierced the air. Kris hugged her belly with one hand and walked beside me.

We stepped over the yarrow and slope, over a drunk and fallen spruce, then let the maw swallow us at the same time. Our shoes sunk into the hot sponge of soil. Tree shadows patterned us, mosquitoes buzzing in and out in rotation.

"I used to come here and smoke Dad's du Mauriers with friends when I was grounded," she said, shooting her shutter at fuzzy bugs trapped in spiderwebs. I slapped a leg and flicked away the pulp.

"I got lost here with Bear," I said. "Mom still says Bear lives on a farm."

"Shit, do I miss Bear. And that's right. I remember when you got lost."

"He spanked me that day. Three years old and guy smacks me on the ass cuz I ended up in the forest while he was supposed to watch me."

"Just remember that you had it easy."

Half an hour in, the trail ended. I boosted Kris over poison ivy and mud. Spotted swamps and other Happyland scabs. Patches of tall grass around muddy water. In winters, our socks soaked whenever the boot broke through the swamp ice.

"Do you remember coming back here that day?" I asked. "It was December. You were with Leeroy and you threatened to run away from the house. Nobody believed you, except me. I tagged along and you brought a little box of Frosted Flakes. You lasted an hour."

Kris had to stop between the fits of belly laughs, and we wandered into an overgrowth of weeds, taking some way I'd never seen before.

"When was the last time you saw Dad?"

"About a year ago or so," I said.

"I saw him the other day."

"How about that. Ever remember what he said when he moved out of the house?"

"That Mom was supposed to take care of us."

"Really? What did Mom say?"

"That Dad was supposed to pay child support."

And then we walked together for some time without saying anything, only the crackle under us breaking the quiet. We went up a hill and hit a road with droning cars heading down the highway. Twenty minutes on the road one way would have taken us to a beach and a trailer park. The other way was Willow Crescent and Eastside Drive, Happyland proper just on the other side.

"Forgot you ended up out here. Let's head back to the car."

We walked to the corner of Soules and Willow.

"Do you remember when I ended up on the news? I ran away because I thought Dad caught me sneaking out with my boyfriend."

"What about Zion?"

"What about him?"

"Ever think about how it was when we were kids and now you're going to be a mom?"

"Been raising you two since I was sixteen. You turned out just fine."

We left muddy footsteps going down Willow Crescent. We giggled a bit with every step. Every house had a satellite dish for reception. I pointed to the house where I pushed a rock into a pond, slaughtering dozens of fish and tadpoles. And then I saw something I didn't notice when we drove in: Caillou's backyard. His playhouse nowhere in sight.

Kris and I continued at the bend, walking right by the house where Bear's puppies were born and stopped for a moment at the pine trees lining the side of it. The junk Ford that Mindi and O Touro had left in the front was gone. The treehouse O Touro never finished was gone.

When we got back in the car, I played "Road to Zion" by Damian Marley on my iPhone.

Kris reversed out the dirt lot and hit the gas. She whipped down Telford Line and joined the rest of Highway 11, away from the Eastside of Happyland as fast as the Acura could take us. I haven't been back since.

Buckle Up

So impatient and in heat I was, agreeing to pledge myself to debt for that first instalment of OSAP at eighteen, earliest a half-bad could sign on for a get-up-and-go fund. No time to wait another two semesters at Patrick Fogarty Catholic to curl a decent graduating average, let alone stay in Sunshine City long enough until next year's applications were due. Never mind that Fairford's education director told me they would have likely funded me in the following year if I managed to hand in my application for assistance on time. Perhaps I could have learned some more hospitality instincts and tricks serving kids their cookie skillets at Brewery Bay. I could have let my wages stretch over a couple years. End my itinerant living. Keep tweeting edgy shit from my laptop and sending horny Facebook messages and texts to my crushes before sneaking them into my bedroom in the middle of the night. Julian would have probably even let me take over his thousand-a-month store-top steal after Laura got pregnant in the summer. An apartment of my own, built on the laminate floorboard that I watched Julian seal in during the summer months, falling asleep shift after bartending shift at Brewery Bay to the harangue of hosers, wannabe surfers, and no-bang gangsters hanging around Sunshine City's main drag. Bet I probably could have found my certain stable in Sunshine City and actually took the time to big think, little do. Or maybe even coast the whole thing all on my lonesome. But I didn't want to wait.

Nothing boosted me like seeing Mindi's and Kris's and Julian's and Laura's smiles when I showed them the acceptance in the most mellow glimmer of evening light, my ticket to the Adventure of Learning. It made Mindi so proud that us three were making our way through the world and so I had to go wherever this took me, no matter how temporally or behaviourally or geographically forward or backward I went.

So I clicked hard into my dinosaur laptop's touchpad and accepted the satellite university's we-don't-want-you-or-your-79-average-but-we'd-still-like-your-money offer, months after everyone else got theirs. I printed the documents at the newly renovated library and crossed at Coldwater Road, hit the bricks all the way to the post office, where I mailed in the form-scrolled and filled-in terms of agreement. Only five minutes to close. Probably the last day I could go, which was also the nicest day of the year.

I didn't care if the university's administration pulled me off the residence wait-list two days before first semester's start date. I didn't care if I had no savings. I wanted in.

I called on O Touro, who agreed to chauffeur me from Kris's place in Barrie to Plaza City. He arrived on the faded gravel lot behind Julian's building later that night, in a brand-new hatchback Explorer, painted red.

Julian and I walked up and down the stairs, tossing some final boxes into the Explorer, while O Touro talked about ending things with a lady in Barrie who was giving him grief. "Can't help it. No point in settling with any of these women anyways."

"Don't know what makes you think we want to hear it," Julian said, unloading my new printer. "Ever think it's not them?"

O Touro slammed the hatch. "Nope. Telling you."

I hadn't seen O Touro since the winter, when he dropped by for a long-overdue visit during the first blizzard of the season. Told us two he was making a living driving out-call escorts to their johns. Waited for them to finish and intervened if needed. O Touro breathed in deep when showing us two his honed-n-toned braggadocio before briefly mentioning he had to get involved to save an out-call every now and then. But never mind that, how you two been? God, would you look at the ceilings in here.

Anybody's guess was better than mine as to how many times O Touro met his heart before shortly sending it on its way. I'd guess somewhere in the forties or fifties, but that's only what I've seen. It was probably more. Few half-bads might say he was born without a heart, found his beat another way, when it came. Then a few years ago he met this sweet little lady who blushed whenever one of us spoke to her about him, told the whole room she waited a long time for someone like O Touro. And one day he invited us to a barbecue in their backyard and asked my sister to bring her camera cuz he had a ring, and this was going to be it. He dressed up in a fresh beige shirt and put a voodoo tie on. He even got down on his knee, and with that back of his you know it meant he loved this one. She cried, which probably meant she loved him. There was nothing like it. But then it was just like everything else.

We finished hauling my hella incomplete university starter pack through the cig-stink hallway, down the white-bulb staircase, and it all began to feel real, and I felt so little with Julian and Laura walking me out, all smiles and goodbyes. I owed them for housing me, feeding me, and caring for me. I owed them for taking me in and then getting a bigger apartment so that I could stop sleeping on the couch. Even when I tried to take out a line of credit, it was Julian who came with me to the Peter Street bank, who shook the man's hand, who offered to be my co-signer, who took me to midnight launches at the Square Mall and Future Shop, who introduced to me one of the few salvageable orders at Pizza Pizza. I hugged them both as hard as I could cuz I couldn't give them much else.

O Touro tossed them two a double-honk on our way out the parking lot and took off for Kris's house in Barrie. Fifteen-minute drive down Highway 11. Zion roamed around the house with a binky in his mouth and got into everything cuz half the place was in boxes.

My sister had enrolled in a photography and digital imaging program in Barrie after earning enough credits to apply. She went back to school for Zion and was getting ready to leave her boyfriend after he pulled too many little thinks for her liking. The two of us split a bottle of wine into two cups to celebrate the learning to come, clinked them to *The Hobbit* movie cuz the road goes ever on, and fell asleep before Bilbo's company embarked on the journey ahead.

The next morning, I emptied my debit and gave O Touro what I had left after the printer and Winners trip. We both hoped that last twenny or so would get us from Barrie to Plaza City and then get O Touro wherever he needed to go. I don't remember asking him or if he told me. I do remember us stopping for gas. And sometime after we hit an incredible stretch of box stores that went on for at least a half-hour with all the traffic.

We hit a bunch of reds and then joined a very long line of vans and SUVs at the institution's entrance. The cars grooved and horn-tooted and every parent was altogether confused about the funnel of intestinal roadways. The road took us along a massive bend around the campus and we drove past a schmancy Inuksuk that pissed a lot of the students off after everybody found out it cost a million bones. Talk about a big do.

We followed the road to a roundabout, and then we found the WELCOME DAY signs. Three, then nine, then twenty-plus cars pulled in behind us to wait in the car-up. Once our section had finally entered the drop-off queue by the apartment building, I was told to head inside and grab my residence card and O Touro was told to head to McLuhan Court.

When I stepped out and into the McLuhan boundary, I was greeted by butterflies, moths, and the don, who told me I'd be living in the middle of the court. Everything was either tanned or warmed by the heat. Students selfied and said farewell to their crying and smiling families outside of their townhouses and in the cafeteria, which was one of seven places undergraduates could take their T-Cards to pay for hot instant meals and order Pizza

Pizza. O Touro had a good laugh when I told him that. No fucking way. Must be nice.

I entered my residence, covered in carpet and filled with the most plywood-looking furniture I'd ever seen. It was clean and painted a faint indigo and all the cabinets were empty.

"Hello?" I said, walking around. "Dad?"

"That you, Cody?" O Touro called out. "Up here."

I went upstairs and found him in my room.

"Keep your toilet paper in the closet. I left the clothes and posters for you to figure out."

"They said I could use my T-Card. It's activated now."

"Do you mind buying a Coke for me? I'll pay you back when we get to the car."

"No need. It's on me."

We sat outside on a bench and O Touro sipped his Coke and I sipped my cocktail fruit juice.

"You know none of this is free, right?"

"I know."

Squirrels climbed the rows of trees, geese hissed and shit freely in the lush turf. It was beautiful. Institution-fed grass lined the campus roads. It was so green I couldn't believe it. Us two walked under giant and sharp buildings that cast shadows below them. We walked past the gym-swim-nasium and arrived at O Touro's Explorer.

"Thanks again for driving, Dad."

"Thanks for the Coke, son. Good luck, bud."

We bear-hugged, said our love-yous, and then I watched his Explorer drive off.

Fly

"You know how nice the house would have been if either of them knew what they were doing?"

"If they knew?" Julian leaned back on his couch with a glass of scotch between his legs and muttered something under his breath. He'd drunk his way to the bottom half of a bottle of premium Johnnie Walker Platinum that'd been stashed in the cupboard since he and Laura found out she was pregnant with son number two, last one out before the vasectomy. "If only they acted smart with their money instead of stupid. I've gone over this with myself many times. The five of us could have had a sustainable life. A fall-back. An inheritance." He sipped from his glass and slipped on an elf hat. He never did drink much.

"I still dream about it constantly," Kris said to attend to Julian's non-Julian outburst. "I want it back."

"Nope," Julian said. "No fucking way. Have nightmares about

that house. In my bedroom and it's barren and I'm deserted. Terrible nightmares. Bad things going on in that house. Always."

"Your bedroom I never dreamed about," she said.

It was Christmas and us three were at Julian's house in a village ten minutes away from Sunshine City and thirty long kilometres from Happyland. We'd spent the evening before having dinner with Mindi and Leacock and Miakoda. Julian worked six days a week at Casino Rama until the early morning to pay for the house. Always saving for a cost-efficient furnace or dishwasher or diapers and other key sundries, always building newer, better benches for his kids so that they can reach the dinner table. Always building new dinner or coffee tables, too. Bookcases. Remodelling the stairs to the basement, complete with safe landings. And sure enough, he'd go on to receive an education as a plumber so he could repair the pipes if they burst, too.

"Because I didn't have one," Julian said. He finished his drink and poured another. He poured my sister a new glass of wine. "House haunted in your dreams, too?"

"I have nightmares sometimes," Kris said. "But I also have not-nightmares."

Kris hadn't stopped working since she graduated at the top of her photography program. She won awards and finished with honours, was brought on to assist in big campaigns, taught Photoshop classes at the college, and began cultivating a growing business. And even with all that, she always made time for her own artistic practice, where she conceptualized surrealist, haunting fantasies and bizarre fairy tales that posed those closest to her as winged and galactic and floating and airy, where Zion blew bubbles through a wand that morphed into planets and my brother walked a dark and stormy road to the blank beyond.

"My room was haunted."

"No, my room was haunted."

"That bathroom between your room and mine was definitely haunted. It was the most awful place in the whole house and it was just wasted. That bathroom stunk like shit and nobody cleaned it. The septic blew and we couldn't use it because the toilet wouldn't flush. It'd be clogged with shit."

"The upstairs one was clogged with shit, too."

"I remember showering in that bathroom for hours."

"How could you? We were on a well. That water went cold too quickly."

"When they were still together, everything in the house ran fine. But when they separated, that's when shit came up."

"Like I said, they did the wrong thing. Instead of fixing up the house and making the place look nice, they bought nice things. They bought everything on credit and ruined it. They had that one white car."

"The Ford."

"That was understandable. But then it crapped out. So he bought that white truck, and then she bought a HondaCR-V. And then he's like, 'Well, if you get a new car then I get a new car.'"

"That CR-V was the car I learned to drive on," Kris said. "And then she got a computer, and then he got a stereo system."

"And then he got The Plasma and those leather couches."

"And then I peed on them," I said.

"That was when she found out what happened to her. Pretty sure she got back forty thousand dollars. It was like winning the lottery. And then they just fucking blew it all."

"It was a manageable mortgage. They could have paid it off like that." Julian snapped his fingers. "With the amount of money the two of them were making in tips, or even when he left the casino and worked at Hydro One . . . They could have had the house paid off in ten fucking years. But no. They kept the payments minimal, remortgaged, and then increased the monthly payments. I don't want to be like them. I don't want to be stupid with money."

"Well, I am sometimes," Kris admitted. "I still go shopping. Clothes, mostly. I think it came from getting made fun of for wearing the same shit. Think it's embedded into the memories."

"I don't worry. I won't buy myself new stuff ever."

"That's why I stole you guys so many new clothes," Kris said. "So you never had to feel what I felt."

"Not like we didn't feel it. I wore the same pair of blue pants and same black shirt and same vest every day. For those two years. I once didn't shower for three months. In high school, I never knew who the dirty kid was."

"Cuz the dirty kid was you," I said.

"But I never went to school for anybody to notice. So it didn't matter anyways."

"Zion!" I called my nephew over to the couch after putting my beer on the ground. We high-fived.

Then Zion started screaming "fly" and morphed into a great big bird, flying around the living room. He flew into the walls and over the oakwood coffee table.

"I remember doing the same thing as him, but I actually flew," Julian said.

"He's probably flying right now but we can't see it."

"No, I'm pretty sure I flew. I was in my Batman costume and I flew a couple feet or so."

"Oh, did you now?"

"I did. But I was looking at myself. I remember seeing myself fly. But then someone walked in the room and I fell. Did you ever do that when you were a kid? Where you just jumped into your imagination and that was the real world, if only for a brief moment?"

Epilogue

HALF-BAD STORY

Your story is the one thing in life that is truly yours.

Story is what red-rovers us to one another, spirit to spirit. Everything has a little bit of story in it, even the changing weather and birdsong, even big team battles and trampoline sessions. Story is what happens when we fall in the thrall of the Play-Doh of it all and feverishly reach for life. Story is what transforms us through the lush valleys of becoming, rolling around in the gutters of raw, pure energy. The afterimage of good living. Story happens when you spear the future tense and embrace yourself for the robot invasions, increasing temperatures, and troll-filled dungeons that the Creator will task you with surmounting, on the roadside trails that open your skin, in the gardens you mend, around fires that spider your hot dogs, in your video game and movie marathons.

Remember that your story is no *Oprah* episode and belongs to no audience or company-turned-country. You have to protect against anyone interfering with the sovereignty of your story and those who make you feel like a Stimpy or a Wiggum or a second-hand Zoboomafoo, especially if the interferer is you.

Never let the distorted realities that make thriving and itinerant survivalists of us all oust you from joy and imagination and from your story. A story born from idiosyncrasy and the infinite singularities of happenstance. Within those infinite singularities of happenstance are capsules of memory stored deep in your bones and in the valves that keep your blood pumping. That make you you.

When we emerge from aki, from the marble of terra, stories about us appear in the minds of those who know us, but also those who don't know us. Many have little time for all the complexities and will seek the most instant, deliverable story they can get out of you. They may even try to tell your story for you. If you let them tell it once, they'll tell it twice, and twice more after that. And if you're not careful, they'll tell it so many times that you'll no longer recognize the story as your own.

So think carefully and be intentional when approaching your story. Fill yourself up with care when you share it with others. Ensure that your toes have care when you jump off the edge of the cliff, over the finish line, onto the train or plane platform. Take every part of your body, your little piggies, your aching ears, and treat them with care. Care takes time and effort. Care is hard work. And thinking carefully is the slowest path you will ever take. Stay gentle with your thinking and dreams and emotions and schemas and they will stay gentle back.

Above all, never forget that thinking little of thinking only leads to the big do, lest you end up like one of those half-bads who tulip their days away thinking the buckle isn't coming. Cuz you need to be ready when it comes. Telling you.

Acknowledgments

Endless gratitude for my family: every immediate and extended member and the generations preceding them. Thanks for "getting it" and for loving um tolo anyways.

Miigwetch to nimaamaa. Thank you for your generosity and encouragement during the writing of this manuscript. For holding things together.

Obrigado to meu pai. Thank you for building community wherever you go, for your commitment to healing, and for telling me.

To Kristine and Julian: thank you for teaching me how to think carefully. To Kristine: you are the first person who encouraged me to write and my most astute reader. To Julian: thank you for the comprehensive feedback on the pipes and for the hordes and hordes of fun.

Thank you to my editor, David Ross, for helping the chicken cross the road. Working with you is a pleasure.

My gratitude to Nicole Winstanley, Kate Sinclair, and Penguin Canada. Thanks to Shaun Oakey for catching those sneaky forces of habit.

Miigwetch to my agent, Stephanie Sinclair, for holding the fort up.

I am grateful for my teachers, especially George Elliott Clarke for pell-mell rhythms, John Currie for psychic space, Kateri Lanthier for missing the shuttle to stay and talk with me after class that one day, Siobhan Matys for believing in this little half-bad from the start, Robert McGill for consecution and mentorship, Robert Price for assonance and cacophony, Shyam Selvadurai for calling my submission promising, and Laurel Waterman for the four virtues.

Miigwetch to Lee Maracle for those eight months together, for making me read the sentences out loud, and for teaching me that stories go looking for people to write them down. For the laughter, the ferocity, and the promise of a title.

My gratitude to the PWC and Life Rattle community: anyone who went to the Totally Unknown Writers Festival, read their story in front of the workshop, or shared an editing circle with me. Much love to Maria E. Cruz, José Guzman, Paige McPhee, and Juliver Ramirez for their early and continued belief.

Thank you to the MA CRW crew: Justin Andrews for taking the late train back to the Hammer, Mary Germaine for the yellow pages, Mitchell Gunn for the insights into video games and literature alike, Zak Jones for every night we coaxed the whirr, Helen Marukh for the tender camaraderie, and Sebastien Wen for lessons on stage and in lyric.

Respect to the Banff squad: Silmy Abdullah, Razielle Aigen,

Elizabeth Aiossa, Shawk Alani, Sarah Berman, Catherine Cockney, Christy-Ann Conlin, Luciana Erregue-Sacchi, Tanis Franco, Jean Hartig, Kerri Huffman, Julie S. Lalonde, Syd Lazarus, Rebecca Morris, Darlene Naponse, Kara Sievewright, Shannon Webb-Campbell, and Jenny Wong. Miigwetch to Liz Howard for the line "That baby minotaur was my truck."

The Avie Bennett Emerging Writers Scholarship, the Interlake Tribal Division for Schools, and the Indspire organization partially funded my education as a writer and the writing of this manuscript. Thanks to Alan Letandre for his administrative support during my university years.

During my undergraduate degree, I would take the UTM shuttle bus downtown to meet a screenwriter named Brad Rochefort in cafés and bakeries, where we charted a path to the first draft. Brad, thanks for your guidance when I still called it *Minotaur*. Thanks as well to Shane Driver, John Dunford, Samantha Haywood, Khashayar Mohammadi, Tamara Wise, and many others for their editorial wit and early feedback on the manuscript. Double thanks to Tamara for giving me a place to write and sip.

The Anishinaabemowin and Portuguese in the book comes from a language learner in his early stages. I've done my best to stick to the regional dialects of Azorean Portuguese and Manitoban/Ontarian Anishinaabemowin, the latter of which is informed by the work of Patricia M. Ningewance. Further gratitude is extended to Eli Baxter, James Vukelich on YouTube, the Ojibwe People's Dictionary. Miigwetch to my uncle Anthony for recommending Patricia and for telling me that bastardized Anishinaabemowin is better than no Anishinaabemowin at all.

CODY CAETANO is a writer of Anishinaabe and Portuguese descent and an off-reserve member of Pinaymootang First Nation. He has an MA in Creative Writing from the University of Toronto, where he wrote this memoir under the mentorship of Lee Maracle. Excerpts of *Half-Bads in White Regalia* earned him a 2020 Indigenous Voices Award for Unpublished Prose.

Fire Exit

Morgan Talty

¶ I wanted the girl to know the truth. I wanted her to know who I was–who I really was–instead of a white man who had lived across from her all her life and watched her grow up from this side of the river.

Finalist for the 2024 Center for Fiction First Novel Prize

Shortlisted for the Maya Angelou Book Award 2024

'In propulsive, spell-binding prose, *Fire Exit* delves into the far-reaching consequences of blood quantum and examines the intersections of familial care and sacrifice. Once again, Talty proves himself witty, wise, and a voice of our age.'

JONATHAN ESCOFFERY

Dear readers,

As well as relying on bookshop sales, And Other Stories relies on subscriptions from people like you for many of our books, whose stories other publishers often consider too risky to take on.

Our subscribers don't just make the books physically happen. They also help us approach booksellers, because we can demonstrate that our books already have readers and fans. And they give us the security to publish in line with our values, which are collaborative, imaginative and 'shamelessly literary'.

All of our subscribers:

- receive a first-edition copy of each of the books they subscribe to
- are thanked by name at the end of our subscriber-supported books
- receive little extras from us by way of thank you, for example: postcards created by our authors

BECOME A SUBSCRIBER, OR GIVE A SUBSCRIPTION TO A FRIEND

Visit andotherstories.org/subscriptions to help make our books happen. You can subscribe to books we're in the process of making. To purchase books we have already published, we urge you to support your local or favourite bookshop and order directly from them – the often unsung heroes of publishing.

OTHER WAYS TO GET INVOLVED

If you'd like to know about upcoming events and reading groups (our foreign-language reading groups help us choose books to publish, for example) you can:

- join our mailing list at: andotherstories.org
- follow us on Twitter: @andothertweets
- join us on Facebook: facebook.com/AndOtherStoriesBooks
- admire our books on Instagram: @andotherpics
- follow our blog: andotherstories.org/ampersand